IT HAD TO
BE YOU

A Dangerous Kiss
With Just One Kiss
A Seductive Kiss
One Night With You
Nobody But You
The Way You Love Me

A Family Affair Series
After the Dawn
When Morning Comes
I Know Who Holds Tomorrow

Against the Odds Series
Trouble Don't Last Always
Somebody's Knocking at My Door

Invincible Women Series
If You Were My Man
And Mistress Makes Three
Not Even If You Begged
In Another Man's Bed
Any Rich Man Will Do
Like the First Time

Standalones
Someone to Love Me
The Turning Point

Anthologies

IT HAD TO BE YOU

Francis Ray

St. Martin's Griffin
New York

Published in the United States by St. Martin's Griffin, an imprint of St. Martin's Publishing Group

www.stmartins.com

ISBN 978-0-312-36507-3 (mass market paperback)
ISBN 978-1-250-08250-3 (trade paperback)
ISBN 978-1-4299-2594-5 (ebook)
ISBN 978-1-250-62405-5 (trade paperback)

First St. Martin's Griffin Edition: April 2020

10 9 8 7 6 5 4 3 2 1

Lovingly dedicated to the dynamic team, Willis Johnson and Alecia Thompson, with the *Willis Johnson Morning Show* on KKDA AM radio in Dallas. Willis, AKA Crooner, never forgets to mention my new titles. Alecia invited me to be the inaugural author with her book club. When I needed a record producer to give authenticity to this book, Alecia located two. Time and time again, they have been there for me whether by having me as a guest on their show or by letting their listeners know my books are available. I deeply appreciate them.

Acknowledgments

Kristie B., recording artist and record producer. Thank you so very much for inviting me into your studio and showing me all the intricacies of making a record. It was fantastic. You are incredibly talented. Please look for her CD.

Michael Smoot, orchestra teacher with the Dallas Independent School District. Your knowledge of different musical instruments is amazing. Your students are blessed to have you.

Rosalyn Story, successful author and violinist with the Fort Worth Symphony Orchestra. You gave me a real feel for why you selected the violin, and why you're so passionate about your music. You play beautifully.

THE TAGGART FAMILY TREE

Bill and Grace Taggart

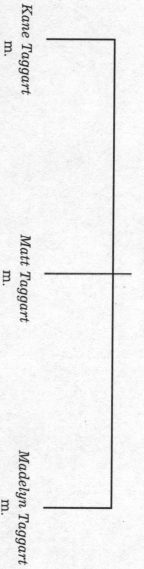

Kane Taggart
m.
Victoria Chandler

FOREVER YOURS

Matt Taggart
m.
Shannon Johnson

ONLY HERS

Madelyn Taggart
m.
Daniel Falcon

HEART OF THE FALCON

One

She haunted him.

There were times when he could think of nothing else. She was passionate one moment, spurning him the next. She drew him, excited him.

And he couldn't have her.

On the telephone in his home office in the hills outside of Los Angeles, Zachary Albright Wilder paced the length of the spacious hickory-paneled room, his anger growing with each agitated step. "What do you mean she won't work with me?" he snapped. "Deliver me from divas."

"Now, Rolling Deep," Oscar Winters, his agent, soothed, using Zach's professional nickname. "Forget this one and move on. After two weeks of not taking my phone calls, I was finally able to corner Laurel Raineau's agent and pull from the sharp-tongued woman that it's your reputation with women and for hard partying that has Raineau backing off. Her agent said that your image isn't the kind she wants associated with her classical music."

"What!" Zachary came to a complete stop

and shoved his hand through the thick, straight black hair that brushed the collar of his shirt. "We're in the twenty-first century for goodness' sake! Sure, I go out with a lot of women, but I'd be suicidal if I was intimate with all of them. I couldn't possibly party as much as the media says or I wouldn't have a wall full of platinum and gold records I've produced."

"Just what I told her agent," Oscar agreed.

"It's not my fault the media chooses to go with what titillates and sells more magazines and newspapers or boosts ratings on the radio or TV rather than the truth," he said, moving across the handwoven silk rug in front of his massive cherry desk. "To have them tell it, I've slept with every female artist I've ever produced, and in my spare time there are the movie starlets and heiresses."

"I tried to tell her agent it was all hype, R.D."

R.D., Rolling Deep, the moniker given to him by one of the first clients he'd ever worked with, a hard-core hip-hop artist whose hero was Scarface. The name stuck as Zach worked with more and more musicians who came from the street—or who wanted people to believe they had.

"Perhaps it's the name." He rubbed the back of his neck. He hadn't thought about it much. To him, the nickname simply meant he didn't have to look to anyone to cover his back. However, he was certain no one feared him. It was the exact opposite. When he went out, he was usually swarmed by autograph seekers or approached by hopeful musicians. He'd changed his cell phone number again just last week because of so many unwanted calls. Twenty-four-hour staffed security at the gated entrance of his home wasn't ego, but necessary to maintain his privacy.

"But your name is known all over the world. You have the golden, or should I say the platinum, touch." Oscar chuckled.

"It seems Laurel Raineau didn't get the memo," he said sarcastically. He'd promised himself long ago that he'd never let his success go to his head. He'd seen it wreak havoc with too many lives. Your star could fall even faster than it rose.

"Forget her," Oscar said again. "In two months you go back into the studio with Satin to do her next album. She was at Mr. Charu's last night and asked about you."

Zach grunted. The restaurant in LA was one of "the" places to be seen. The very reason Zach seldom went there anymore. Satin had the voice of an angel and the sexual appetite of a succubus. While working with her on her last album he'd flatly told her that if she didn't stop coming on to him, he was walking. He had never been intimate with a client and he didn't intend to start.

He should just move on as Oscar said, but he couldn't. Despite her snobbish attitude, when Laurel Raineau picked up a violin, it was pure magic. The music drew you, moved you. Passion and fire.

Laurel was five foot three and probably weighed

110 pounds soaking wet with all of her clothes on. Yet her music was more powerful than any he had ever heard, and he'd listened to and played musical instruments for as long as he could remember.

For personal and professional reasons he wanted to produce her next album. As a free agent, he was in a position to pick and choose his projects. There was a long list of musical entertainers from every genre who wanted to work with him.

All except Laurel Raineau. That stopped today. "Did you get her address?"

"I did," Oscar answered, relief in his voice that he had been able to do at least one thing his biggest client had asked. "It's a couple of miles from you, actually." He gave him the address.

Zach was moving behind his desk before his agent finished. "Hold." He pressed the intercom to the garage. "Toby, bring the car around immediately."

"Be right there, Zach."

Toby Yates, friend, former drag car racer, and chauffeur, was one of the few people who called Zachary by his name. "Talk to you later, Oscar."

"If you took no for an answer, you wouldn't be where you are today. Bye."

Zachary disconnected the call and headed for the front door. Ms. Snob wouldn't find it so easy to ignore him. She'd have to tell him to his face all the crap she'd said about him—if she had the courage.

Opening the twelve-foot door, Zachary quickly went down the fourteen steps to the waiting black Bentley. Toby was there with the back door open, as Zach had known he'd be.

"Thanks." Zachary practically dove inside. He didn't need a chauffeur most of the time, but there were occasions when he was working on a song, was too tired after seemingly endless hours in the recording studio, or was with a client who he didn't want to drive. It also gave Toby a reason to stick to his sobriety. He'd been with Zach ever since Zach came to LA against his father's wishes to make a name for himself in the music industry.

Zach's fist clenched. He'd done what he'd set out to do, but the rift between him and his father was never mended before his death.

The car pulled off smoothly and started down the long drive. The iron gates swung open. He gave Toby the address. He wouldn't need a GPS system. He'd grown up in LA and knew the streets well.

In a matter of minutes Toby turned up a steep hill that gradually leveled off. Up ahead was the ambiguous iron gate. Zach felt a muscle leap in his jaw. Toby pulled up until the back window of the car was even with the speaker box.

Zach rolled down the window and punched the black button. "Zachary Wilder to see Ms. Raineau."

"Ms. Raineau is unavailable."

Zachary held on to his temper. It wouldn't do

any good to blow. The person was just following orders. "Perhaps if you'd tell her who is calling, she might change her mind."

"The answer would be the same" came the droll reply.

Patience. "If you would please just tell her."

"Sir. She is unavailable and this conversation is over."

Zachary locked the curse behind his lips. If he ever got his hands on Ms. Snob, he'd have a few choice words with her. He sat back in his seat. "Home."

Toby pulled off and started back down the road. Arms folded, Zachary slumped back in his seat. Somehow, some way, he was going to talk to her.

"Zach, a stretch limo just came out of the gate."

Zach shot up in his seat. Sure enough, there was a black limo behind them. The car could have dropped her off or anyone else off or have someone else inside. "Once we're on the street, follow it and don't let it get away."

Toby snorted, straightened his mirror. "You're such a kidder."

Zach grinned. Toby lived for speed. He might not have a GPS system, but he did have the latest radar detector.

The limo passed, and although Zach already knew he wouldn't be able to see inside, he leaned closer to the window. "Can you tell if it's a car service or private?"

"Service," Toby answered.

The chances went up that Laurel might be in the car. People who were as successful as she usually had a personal driver. They tended to be more loyal and they were on hand whenever you needed them, but Laurel hadn't been in LA long enough to hire a driver.

"He's taking the exit to LAX."

Better and better. Zachary watched the limo take the lane for departing international flights. "Ten bucks says Ms. Snob is in that car."

"Not this time," Toby said good-naturedly. "I always lose when I bet with you."

Laughing, sensing he'd run Laurel to ground at last, Zach scooted forward in the backseat. "I've got you now."

"The paparazzi are always hanging out here. You're going to have to be fast on your feet to get past them," Toby warned.

As a part member of a chart-topping band, and now a producer for many of the top musical stars, he received a lot of attention.

Zach had always been courteous in the past. It was better that way. However, today he had no intention of letting the horde with cameras and mikes slow him down.

The limo inched its way over to the curb and parked. Toby muscled the Bentley in ahead of a Jaguar. The man in the car laid on his horn in protest. "You better hurry. I'll circle."

Zach was already reaching for the door handle. On the sidewalk he hurried toward baggage check-in for first-class passengers. He didn't see her until a guy who looked like he could bench-press five hundred pounds and not break a sweat moved to reveal a delicately shaped woman wearing large-rimmed sunglasses, a short-brimmed woven hat edged with black ribbon, a white blouse, and slim black pants. On the other side of her was a twin to the first guy.

Laurel Raineau. Victory. Grinning, Zach moved to follow her into the terminal. He made it within five feet of her before one of the twin samurai faced him, blocking his way. He moved to step around him. The man moved with him.

"You're in my way," Zachary said.

The man said nothing.

Zachary tried to look past or over him, but that was impossible. He was a yard wide. "Should I call airport security?"

The bodyguard folded his massive arms.

"Rolling Deep!" a female voice screeched. "It's Rolling Deep!" The cry was taken up by another and another. If he had miraculously managed to escape the attention of the paparazzi earlier, he was in for it now.

A crowd converged on him. Cameras flashed. The bodyguard moved back, then turned and walked away. There was no way Zach could continue. People would follow. If he got close to her again, her bodyguards would stop him. He was sure security was nearby, watching to see that things remained relatively calm.

All he'd need was Laurel seeing him having an altercation with the authorities. She already thought the worst of him. Swallowing his disappointment, he signed any paper and legal body parts presented to him.

Laurel had managed to escape him.

Later that night, on the balcony of his house, Zachary stood with a bourbon glass in his hand and gazed out at the sprawling lights of Los Angeles below. He'd purchased the home a couple of years ago for the view and the isolation. Sometimes he needed to get away, and Cliff House, as he'd come to call his home, allowed him to do just that.

He needed both tonight. He'd been a few feet away from Laurel and hadn't been able to talk with her. No one probably had. He didn't think it was because her two scary bodyguards would deter a real autograph hound.

The mere fact that she had bodyguards should have put the media and the autograph seekers on full alert. That hadn't happened. Her last album, as had all the rest, might have gone platinum, but her audience wasn't the screaming, in-your-face type wanting you to sign their bodies.

He had nothing against his fans. They just expressed their pleasure in different ways. Pity. Laurel might be snobbish, but her music deserved to be heard by the masses.

And she thought him beneath her. Just as his own father had. Zach's hand clenched the glass. His father had called the hip-hop and pop music he produced "useless noise."

Having a man you looked up to dismiss your passion, hurt. They'd never managed to get past their differences. At the time of his father's death, they were still estranged.

Perhaps that was one of the reasons Zachary wanted to produce Laurel's next album. His father had loved classical music. Oddly, it was her music that soothed and touched Zach more than anything else after his father's death.

Zachary had been working late one night—at least trying to—when he'd heard the haunting sound of a violin. He'd looked up from the keyboard to the large-screen TV he'd forgotten he had on.

Her dark head was bent, her eyes half closed, her lips slightly parted as if held in the grip of passion. He'd risen and walked closer to the fifty-two-inch screen and just stood there, mesmerized by the sounds she seemed to effortlessly coax from her instrument. She was a stunning combination of cool beauty and gut-wrenching passion. Her black hair was drawn away from a knock-out face with ice-pick cheekbones, full lips, and a dainty nose. Her floor-length ball gown had been eye-popping red.

He'd reached for the remote control and hit RECORD, chastising himself for being so slow to react. Once her segment was over he'd booted up his computer, found her Web site, and purchased all seven of her albums. They were good, but he'd always felt that she had held back. He suspected that, like many musical artists, Laurel performed better in front of a live audience. Her producer should have understood and worked to get her to bring that same incredible fire to the studio.

The idea of him being that producer had taken root when he'd read that she had rented a home in LA to work on her next album. But she wanted nothing to do with him. He sipped his drink. Somehow, some way, he'd change her mind. Like Oscar said, a *no* didn't deter him.

Behind Zachary, the phone on his nightstand rang. Ice cubes clinked against the crystal as he sipped his iced tea. In the old, foolish days he'd let everyone believe it was bourbon. Those days of trying to fit in or impress people were long gone. Now people tried to impress him.

Except one beautiful woman.

"Hello, Zachary. You didn't return my call last week. I really need to talk to you. Call me."

Zachary took another sip and thought about dumping his tea and adding the real deal. These days Carmen could try the patience of a saint. She was too clingy, too needy, and perpetually in a funky mood. A lifetime ago she had tossed the engagement ring he'd bought her back in his face and stomped on his pride with her stiletto heels. He'd been just out of college and ready to conquer the world. She'd given him a fast reality check.

They had been lovers for six months. He'd thought she loved him as much as he loved her, and would gladly follow him to LA. He was wrong. She thought he was crazy for planning to go off on his own and leave his privileged life behind. She had no intention of going with him and be bored or do without while he tried to start a music career.

Carmen hadn't left her name on the answering machine, wouldn't have thought she had to. At thirty, beautiful, willful, pampered—she would hate the more accurate word, *spoiled*—she thought the world revolved around her. Her older husband and the fluctuating economy were giving her a reality check of her own.

The word in their circle of friends in Atlanta was that Carmen wasn't adjusting well to her husband's financial woes. They'd moved to a smaller home, let their house staff go, were down to two cars instead of five, and were no longer members of the country club. Since her parents, who had always catered to their only child, had invested in her husband's business ventures, they were in the same sinking boat.

Zach and Carmen had met again at a party when he'd gone home for Christmas. They hadn't seen each other since that night. She'd tearfully apologized for her behavior and begged him to forgive her. Because he'd long since moved on and was happy with life, he didn't see any reason to hold a grudge.

She'd asked for his phone number to keep in touch and, because she'd looked so miserable, kept dabbing at the tears in her eyes, and was so unlike the fun-loving woman he once wanted to marry, he'd given it to her. Since then she'd called every couple of weeks. He usually called her back the next day, but he wasn't in the mood to hear again how unfair life was. He probably shouldn't have given her his new number.

He had his own sob story.

The answering machine clicked on. If that was Carmen again, he really was getting bourbon.

"Hi, Zach. I just called to say I love you and bug you about visiting us again."

Zachary turned at the animated sound of his younger sister's voice. These days each time he heard Paige's voice, she sounded happier than the last time. Marriage and Shane Elliott agreed with her. He moved toward the phone.

"Mother is coming for the weekend again." Bright laughter drifted over the answering machine. "She lives ten minutes away, but Shane insists that she stay over. She's helping us design the garden rooms. Shane and I both like having her around."

Zach picked up the phone, his mouth curving into a smile. "Hi, Sunshine."

"Hi, yourself. When are you coming for a real visit?"

"I was just there for Christmas," he reminded her as he walked back onto the terrace.

"It's April, Zach," she told him. "You work too hard."

"I haven't been to the studio in weeks," he admitted.

"Are you all right? Is anything the matter?" she asked, worry creeping into her voice.

"Fine," he quickly assured her. For as long as he could remember, music had been a part of his life. He ate, slept, and dreamed music. His near obsession was one of the many reasons he and his father hadn't gotten along.

"This is your sister who watched you master instrument after instrument, the sister who you first told you were going to Juilliard instead of Stanford as Father wanted because you couldn't imagine a life without music," Paige reminded him. "Come clean. Or do I have to ask Shane to find the answer for me?"

Zach shook his head at the new assertive Paige. She had come into her own since Shane. He straightened as a thought struck. "Is Shane as good an investigator as you think?" he asked.

"He's the best or he wouldn't have been head of security for Blade Navarone or so quickly made a name for himself with his own firm here in Atlanta," she said proudly. "So talk."

"It's a woman," he began slowly, wondering how to explain without sounding as if he'd gone around the bend.

"You've finally fallen in love," Paige said, excitement ringing in her voice.

"No, no," he quickly said. He wasn't going down that dead-end road again. "Nothing like that. Laurel Raineau is a concert violinist, one of the best in my opinion, and I've been trying to get her to let me produce her next album. But

I'm hitting a stone wall in trying to talk to her. She left this afternoon on an international flight."

"You won't need Shane for this," Paige said.

He frowned. "What?"

"Laurel's sister, Sabra, is married to Pierce Grayson. Pierce is Sierra's brother and, as you know, she's married to Blade. You met Sierra and Blade at my wedding. He and Rio were Shane's best men. Rio has been head of Blade's personal and professional security since Shane resigned, but he, Blade, and Shane are still best friends."

Zach placed his drink on the stone-topped table to massage his temple. "I'm trying to follow you."

She laughed. "I heard Shane laughing and talking to Blade about Rio's temporary assignment and, although you can't tell what he's thinking, they knew he hadn't liked it one bit. It had something to do with Laurel. I'll ask Shane if he knows where she is."

"Could you please?" Zach said. "For a town where nothing is a secret, no one seems to know her location."

"Rio's doing. I can't imagine anyone with an ounce of sense wanting to go against or anger him," Paige said.

"I seem to remember at your wedding rehearsal, you standing toe-to-toe with him," Zach said. He'd thought he'd have to rescue her. Instead Rio had dipped his head in acceptance and walked away.

"Oh, that," Paige said in a dismissive tone. "He

knows I love Shane, so we're all right. Like Shane and Blade, he's fiercely loyal. No matter what's going on, they manage to get together every month or so. It's kind of hectic, scheduling it around all of our jobs, but since Sierra and I don't want to be left behind, we manage. We promised when we married that we would never be apart at night. Blade and Sierra made the same promise."

That was the close, can't-do-without-you way marriages should be, Zach thought. His parents never had that kind of relationship. His father spent a lot of nights away from home, but his mother never complained. She was the most incredible woman in the world and, no matter what, she was always there for him and Paige, cheering them on, encouraging them. She was proud of him and took every opportunity to tell him.

"You have powerful friends." Blade Navarone was a billionaire, and word on the street was that neither he nor any of his family or friends was to be messed with. Shane and Rio received the same wide-eyed deference.

"I just think of them as friends."

That was Paige, unselfish, loyal, and down-to-earth. She hadn't had many friends growing up, but she had certainly made up for it since.

"Hold on, Shane is in his study."

Zach paced as he waited. In a matter of seconds she was back.

"Laurel is at Navarone Riviera Maya, Blade's private resort in Playa del Carmen. She's staying in one of the luxury condos Blade decided to keep for friends and family who wanted to visit," Paige told her brother.

"Thank you. That's a four-hour plane ride from here," Zachary said. "I'll call my travel agent and see if she can get me a flight out ASAP. A hotel might be more of a problem."

"No, it won't. It's already taken care of," Paige said. "I asked Shane if there were any other vacancies there. As one of the perks, Shane and now Rio have a place to stay at all of Blade's properties while they check on security. Shane is going to call Rio, but he's sure it's all right if you use the house, a cottage, at the back of Blade's estate."

Zach laughed out loud. "Little sister to the rescue."

"You've always been there for me," she said with meaning. "It's about time I returned the favor."

"You have, countless times in the past," Zach told her. She'd tried so hard to mend the rift between him and their father, often at the expense of their father getting upset with her. She'd idolized their father, and those confrontations were always hard on her. He'd finally told her to stop trying. "Please tell Shane thanks."

"I will," she said. "I love Laurel's music. I've never heard her in person, but I know of her, and of course her famous Broadway sister, Sabra. I've yet to meet Sabra or Pierce. They were in New

York when Shane and I flew to Santa Fe last month to meet Blade and Rio for one of their meetings."

"Laurel is beautiful, brilliant, and elusive," Zach said. "Now that I know where she is, I can persuade her to let me produce her next album."

"If anyone can, you will. But I understand Sabra said Laurel wanted some undisturbed downtime, and, although you won't see a bodyguard, you can be sure that Rio will make sure she isn't bothered."

Zach rubbed the full beard he'd enjoyed wearing for the past three years. He'd never liked shaving every day. "One look at me and she'll probably sic her guard on me." He told her about the airport incident.

"Not if you tell her that you're practically family," Paige said. "I told you, Sierra is Sabra's sister-in-law. They're really close. Family means a lot to all of them, just like it does to us."

Paige's idea had merit, but she didn't know how Laurel felt about him. If she recognized him, it would be all over. His hand went to the full beard he'd cultivated for the past three years. "You saved me from another restless night. I'll grab the first flight I can get."

"Let me know if you have any trouble getting to her. I'll ask Shane to call Rio."

The last thing he wanted was for Rio or Shane to tell Laurel who he was before she had a chance to get to know him and see that all the crazy stories about him weren't true. "Thanks, but I can handle it from here."

"Then you owe me a visit," she bargained.

He chuckled. "All right. I'd planned to come down Mother's Day weekend."

"Great. 'Night, Zach."

" 'Night, Sunshine." Zach hung up the phone and started from the room to shave off his beard. *Laurel Raineau, here I come. For the sacrifice I'm about to make you had darn well better listen to what I have to say.*

Two

Laurel Raineau, you should have never allowed Sabra to talk you into this trip.

Laurel sighed and reached for the glass of white wine she didn't want. She'd ordered it with her dinner at the sommelier's suggestion. She sipped it now as an excuse to remain in the posh restaurant instead of going back to her luxurious but lonely room.

She should have just stayed at her rental property in Los Angeles. Even as the thought formed, she knew that if she had, her mother would never have gone to her high school's fortieth reunion in Louisville. They were almost inseparable. This was the first time since Laurel was sixteen that she was on her own and away from her family.

She might be twenty-six, but she supposed she'd lived a sheltered life. She'd been playing the violin since she was five. The countless hours of daily practice hadn't left much room for other activities or friends. She'd begun touring after she graduated from high school, but even before then there were events and competitions. Her room and the den at her parents' home in Nashville were filled with trophies and awards. And on every trip her mother had been there.

Laurel took another sip and glanced around. Couples were seated at every table. The lone exceptions were two women dining together, and herself.

Shortly after she'd arrived at the restaurant, two men had tried to pick her up, but she'd promptly sent them on their way. She hadn't thought when she'd decided to accept Sierra Navarone's invitation, at Sabra's urging, that the resort would have so many couples.

She fought another sigh. Just what she didn't need—another reminder that she was alone. It was a thought that had occurred more and more frequently since Sabra had married Pierce Grayson.

Laurel wasn't jealous—exactly—but being around the Grayson family and their spouses had a way of making you wish there were someone in your life who looked at you as if he'd be lost without you, as if you were the other part of him.

Tears glittered in her eyes, but she hastily brushed them away. Her father had looked at her mother that way. He would have done anything to ensure her happiness, to ensure the happiness of his "girls" as he fondly referred to them. Her mother wasn't as open or demonstrative as her father, but she loved just as deeply. His sudden death had shaken all of them.

For once, Laurel's music hadn't been able to soothe her. Nothing could ease the jagged hole in her heart. It had been more than a year since his death, and they were slowly moving on. It was time. Her father wouldn't have wanted them to continue to grieve. He'd taught them to live each day to the fullest.

She couldn't recall him ever looking sad except the time he'd come back from a business trip to Santa Fe. She thought it was because his investment business wasn't doing well. Her mother had never worked, and he was their sole provider. In a week or so, however, he'd been his old happy self, and they were on their way to San Francisco for a family vacation.

Laurel thought it appropriate that Sabra had found Pierce, the man of her dreams and heart, in Santa Fe. They were crazy about each other. Sabra divided her time among marriage, Broadway, and acting. She was ecstatically happy and content, and always put Pierce first, just as he did her. Again, Laurel wondered what it would be like to love and be loved that much.

She was probably doomed to not find out anytime soon. Her hectic schedule didn't leave much time for dating. The last time she had dated, it had ended in total disaster and humiliation. Sean Conner had completely conned her. If she let herself think about it too much, she'd get angry and feel gullible and stupid all over again. He was out of her life.

She was in a beautiful resort on the Mexican Caribbean. She should be enjoying herself instead of thinking about a selfish jerk. She ruthlessly pulled her mind from the painful past, thought of her mother, and smiled. She had been so excited when Laurel had seen her off at the airport with two of her friends for their high school reunion.

Helen and Esther had been her mother's best friends all through high school in Louisville. They were determined that she not miss the fortieth reunion as she'd missed all the rest. They still lived there and had flown to Los Angeles to personally persuade her. As if they were still in high school, the three had stayed up and talked most of the night.

Sabra arrived with Pierce the next day to add her encouragement for her mother to go. Pierce had produced three first-class tickets to Louisville and hotel reservations for her mother. They all agreed her mother needed to get away and have time for herself instead of putting all of her time and energy into Laurel. Laurel had just finished a 104-city international tour the month before.

When her mother had expressed concern about Laurel being alone, Sabra had come up with the idea of Laurel taking her own vacation. She'd described Navarone Riviera Maya, with its pristine white sand beaches and the soothing turquoise water of the Caribbean, and Laurel had felt a longing she hadn't been aware of.

With one phone call to Sierra Grayson Navarone, Sabra had everything planned. She'd helped her mother pack, then took Laurel shopping for beachwear. There had been no stopping her. Pierce had just smiled and helped carry all of the bags to the waiting car. All Laurel had to do was walk out the door—this time without her violin. Sabra again. She thought Laurel would spend her days in her room playing instead of having fun.

Laurel's lips twitched. Sabra was probably right. If she had her instrument, she'd be in her room now. She'd toyed with the idea of asking her agent to send it by courier, then dismissed it. She loved her music, but she shouldn't let it be her entire focus in life. Sabra had found a balance, and so would Laurel.

When she returned, she was going into the studio to record her new album. The last one had gone platinum, as had the six previous. Laurel's hand trembled just the tiniest bit. She placed her glass on the table.

Her agent and the executives at her recording label seemed to think it was a foregone conclusion that this album would go platinum as well. She had the same backup musicians, the same producer. Laurel wasn't as optimistic, but she never was while recording.

She loved performing in front of a live audience, feeling connected with them. Hearing the final cuts for the album, the thought always nagged her that something was missing.

Then, too, this would be the first album since she'd lost her father. He wouldn't be there to call her every night and ask her how the day went, encourage her when nothing had seemed to go right, praise her when magic had happened between her and her violin. Tears crested in her eyes. She blinked them away.

She supposed she should go back to her room, but the idea had no appeal. It was luxuriously furnished, beautifully decorated in white and black, had an infinity pool, and was a short distance from the sea, but Laurel felt even lonelier there.

She'd thought being around people would help. It hadn't, and neither had the brief shopping trip this morning along La Quinta Avenida, the main pedestrian walkway. She wasn't sure she could stand seven more days of this. At the last minute, her mother had decided to extend her trip since Laurel was going away as well. Perhaps she could just go home and not tell anyone.

There was only one problem: Rio Sanchez, dark, dangerous, stoic. His eyes were as black as midnight and as sharp as a razor blade. Rio had flown back yesterday in the private jet that had brought them to Cancún, but he'd left a man to guard her.

Somewhere unseen, Kyle Saunders watched her. Laurel had tried to tell Sabra that a bodyguard wasn't necessary, but no one had listened.

She had barely kept from laughing when she'd seen the two men who'd accompanied her to the airport. They talked little. Their eyes moved constantly. While she had fans, they were not as demonstrative as those in the pop industry.

She made a face. She didn't want that kind of notoriety or the bad press. And if she allowed Rolling Deep to produce her next album, she could just imagine what it would do to her image. Even the name conjured up danger, weapons, and hard partying.

She'd heard nothing but sordid stories about him since she'd moved to Los Angeles a couple of weeks ago. She'd told her agent that under no circumstances did she want anything to do with the man. His agent had acted as if she should be honored. She wasn't. There was no way in hell that she'd let him produce her next album.

"Please excuse me, Ms. Raineau, there is a gentleman diner who would like to share your table, if you don't mind?" the maître d' asked. "We have no free tables and we're booked solid."

Laurel looked up at the elegant, olive-skinned tuxedoed man, who appeared a bit uneasy. She tried to decide if the man he spoke of was trying a new pickup line or was in earnest. She didn't have to think for long. The Seascape was located on Navarone property. Guests were afforded luxury and privacy. She reached for her clutch. "He can have—"

"Excuse me for not waiting, but I was afraid you'd say no and I'm starving."

Laurel glanced up. Her breath snagged, her heart did a crazy jitterbug. Staring down at her with the most incredible light brown eyes was a man straight out of a woman's naughty fantasy. Clean-shaven, he was incredibly handsome with dimples he probably hated, a straight nose, a sensual mouth, and straight black hair that brushed the jacket of his beautifully tailored beige silk sport coat.

He extended his hand. It was large, the nails manicured. No rings, but the square-faced, eighteen-karat gold watch with the major cities on the facing was sinfully expensive. "Zachary Albright. I promise I'm harmless."

Automatically she lifted her hand, a bit mesmerized by the sexy grin that made her stomach muscles tighten. There was no way a man this handsome with such teasing grin would ever be harmless. Lethal, definitely. The brief handshake proved her right.

The jolt went straight to her toes in her four-inch black high-vamp sling backs. Since she was barely five-three, she always wore heels when she went out. Shoes, she was serious about.

"Please," he coaxed, his voice a deep rumble that reminded her of moonlight and magic. His long fingers curled over the top of the chair facing her. She could almost imagine them curving around her neck, bringing her lips closer.

"Madam?" the maître d' asked.

She should say no. This man made her body act totally out of character.

"Please," he urged, stepping around the chair to bring himself closer. The impact was immediate. He made every one of her nerve endings go on full alert and pant for mercy.

Run, Laurel, a small voice warned. To where? A lonely room and then what?

"Of course." It was the courteous thing to do. Besides, it would give her someone to talk to for a bit. A flimsy excuse, but it was the best one she could think of with her normally intelligent brain fogged.

"Thank you. I was thinking you'd send me on my way. I just arrived and was afraid I'd have to wait until morning for a decent meal." He laughed, a silken sound that stroked her. She blinked.

What was the matter with her? Lonely or not, she'd never reacted so physically to a man. She hadn't known she could. She had thought all the talk of instant attraction was wishful lies. Even with the user, Sean, she'd been flattered more than aroused when they'd first met. Her feelings for him hadn't gone much deeper. Perhaps that was why it had been so easy to see through his lies.

This man rang all of Laurel's bells, as her hairdresser, Tiffany, would say. Happily married with a husband who adored her, Tiffany often said there was nothing wrong with admiring a good-looking man.

This man took the seat closest to her. The maître d' placed his napkin across his lap. The waiter and sommelier rushed over. The man turned to her. "What would you like?"

Her heart to stop racing, for a start. "Nothing, thank you."

"Then you've eaten dinner?" he asked, seeming unconcerned that the two hovered over him. Apparently he was used to people waiting on him instead of the other way around.

"Yes," she answered a bit reluctantly. For some odd reason she didn't want him to know she had stayed because she was lonely. "I was just finishing my wine."

"Dessert?"

"Nothing," she told him, picking up her wineglass, surprised to find it almost empty.

"Would you like coffee, another glass of wine, or something else?" he persisted.

"Tonic water would be fine."

He nodded his dark head and turned to give his food and their drink order. Finished, he smiled at her. Her heart did a dance again.

Embarrassment battled with the relief that he hadn't been giving her a line. She was so tired of people lying or trying to use her. The more successful she became, the more it seemed people wanted something out of her. It would be wonderful just to be liked as plain Laurel Raineau.

"Is there a problem?"

Laurel's gaze jumped to Kyle's broad shoulders, his intimidating stance, his stoic face. But he wasn't looking at her. His focus was on the man at her table.

Zachary didn't seem concerned. His face pleasant, he stuck out his hand. "Zachary Albright."

The unbending stare wavered, then morphed into a cordial smile. Her security man extended his own hand. "Kyle Saunders. Enjoy your evening."

Laurel was relieved, but a bit surprised by the smile and Kyle's quick departure. He had appeared out of nowhere when the men tried to pick her up earlier. She hadn't been sure if it was her refusal or Kyle's presence that had made them leave the restaurant so quickly. Apparently Kyle approved of her new dinner companion. She certainly did.

"Your wine, sir. Tonic water, miss." The waiter placed the glasses and poured Laurel's water. "Your food will arrive shortly. Your salad and bread are on the way."

"Thanks." Zachary picked up his glass, tipped it toward her. "To a gracious lady, Miss . . ."

She blushed. She hadn't been able to help herself. No one had ever stared at her so intently. At least, no one as incredibly handsome as her unexpected guest. "Raineau, Laurel Raineau."

"You saved a weary traveler, Laurel Raineau. Pleased to meet you." He sipped and then put his glass aside.

"You just arrived?" she asked, trying to relax, but it was difficult with him so close. She was pleased that he'd never heard of her. She could smell his aftershave, a woodsy fragrance mixed with his own masculine scent. Her nostrils actually twitched.

"Straight from the Cancún airport. I dropped

my luggage off and came directly here. I heard the food and service were excellent," he told her. "I promised myself that I wouldn't even think of business for the next eight days. I plan to relax and have fun."

"Your salad, bread, and swordfish, sir." The waiter placed the food on the table. "Pepper or anything else?"

"This should do it." He bowed his head for a few seconds and then picked up his fork. "I'm too starved to wait for separate courses. How long have you been here?"

"I arrived last night." He had perfect white teeth.

"I can't wait to see it in the morning." He ate his food and stared at her. "Is it as breathtaking as I've heard?"

The way he looked at her, the inflection of his voice, sent goose bumps skipping over Laurel's skin. She'd always admired her agent and music execs who could talk and eat at the same time without seeming impolite. That took practice. He was probably a businessman, and he was also a very tempting man. Too tempting.

She picked up her clutch. "I'll leave you to enjoy your meal."

His fork clattered to his plate. "No, please. Don't go. I hate to think I ran you off."

He had, but not in the way he thought. "You haven't. I was about to go. I was just enjoying my wine." She stood.

He immediately came to his feet, his dark eyes narrowed on her face. "Laurel, please stay."

More goose bumps. Her heart fluttered at the sound of her name on his lips. She'd never hear it in moonlight, then feel his mouth on hers. Maybe she reacted so strongly to a perfect stranger because of all her thoughts about couples and realizing she wanted that special connection for herself. She wanted what her parents had.

She swallowed the sudden lump in her throat, battled tears. Memories of her father came rushing back. She'd always thought there would be more time for her to be with him. He and Sabra did things together, but if Laurel wasn't practicing, she was on tour. There never seemed to be any free time. Now she had time, and he wasn't there to share it with her.

"What's the matter?" Zachary asked.

She shook her head, hoping she could get out of the restaurant before the tears fell.

Zachary quickly pulled enough money from his wallet to more than cover the bill. "Let's get out of here." He didn't wait for an answer. Placing his hand in the small of her back, he guided her toward the front door.

Kyle was suddenly there. His sharp gaze flickered from Laurel's strained face to Zachary's implacable one.

"She needs some air," Zach explained.

"You were vouched for. He wouldn't like it if

he were wrong," Kyle murmured, then stepped aside.

Zachary could give a flip about Kyle's veiled threat. All he could think about was getting Laurel out of here. She was trembling all over. One moment she was staring at him with interest, the next she was close to tears.

"Come on, Laurel." They continued out of the restaurant and on to the curved walkway that connected the other businesses of Navarone Resort and Spa.

He saw a sign that pointed to the beach and gently urged Laurel down the well-lit path. He smelled the salty air, saw the numerous palm trees bordering the beach before he heard the waves. Fifty feet farther, the moon-draped sea lay in front of them.

Removing his jacket, he spread it on the sugary white sand. "Let's just sit here for a moment and enjoy the view."

"I-I can't sit on your jacket," she said, her voice the barest whisper.

"I'm certainly not letting you sit on the sand in evening clothes. Besides," he said with a smile, "I've always wanted to rescue a damsel. My sister loved for me to read her fairy tales when she was growing up."

Her arms wrapped around her, Laurel looked out to the sea. "Do you have a large family?"

"Just my mother and sister now," he answered. He hadn't planned to talk about family, just as he didn't want to talk about his business. There were too many chances to slip up.

Laurel swung back around, the glitter of tears thankfully gone from her incredible eyes. "I sort of liked fairy tales myself."

Zachary caught Laurel's arm, felt the fragile bones beneath. She barely reached the middle of his chest. He wanted to draw her to him, fight her dragons for her. His reaction didn't surprise him. Although they'd just met, he felt close to her.

Perhaps that was the reason he'd been so annoyed with her when she refused to see him. He needed her, admired her, and she didn't give a flying fig about him. Her music lulled him to sleep, haunted his dreams, played on his iPod, in his car. "Sit down, and I'll tell you."

Her tempting mouth curved upward. In silky black evening pants, she gracefully sank to his coat.

He stared down at her as she looked up at him. Moonlight suited her. His body tightened fiercely. Lust blindsided him. He could too easily imagine kissing those lips, leaning her back on the sand as his body covered hers.

He quickly sat before she saw his misshapen pants, and told her his little sister's love of fairy tales and how she'd wanted a fairy-tale wedding, without using Paige's name.

Paige knew the family connections because she was married to Shane who, as former head of security, knew all the extended family members connected to Blade. Obviously Laurel didn't—which worked in Zachary's favor. However, he wasn't taking a chance that she might know Rolling Deep was the nickname for Zachary Wilder. Only his lawyer knew his legal name was Albright.

Arriving at the Cancún International Airport he'd been even more grateful for the connection to Shane. There had a vehicle waiting and the key to a cottage at the back of Blade Navarone's home. Zachary had driven the Jeep back to the Seascape, where he had dinner reservations.

He'd hurried to the restaurant, hoping Laurel would be eating there as well. He'd spotted her sitting alone and saw it as his chance to meet her. He'd asked the maître d' to seat him with her and had been quickly refused. Zachary told the stern-faced man that he was Shane's brother-in-law. His resistance had faded like smoke in the wind.

Zachary had watched Laurel from a distance. He'd seen the unmistakable sadness in her stunning face, and he had wanted to take it away and make her smile. He thought his first reaction on seeing her would be anger mixed with satisfaction that he had finally run her to ground. Now he just wanted never to see tears in her eyes again.

He finished by saying, "She loves fiercely and is loyal beyond belief. She's married now and calls her husband her Black Knight. She deserves every moment of happiness she has."

"I hope she never forgets and takes it for granted."

His arm curved automatically around her shoulders. She felt fragile. "You lost someone close to you?"

She shivered. "My father."

"I'm sorry." Of course he had known about her father's death. There had been pain and loss in her live music, her face, since then. He brushed an errant strand of lustrous black hair from her face.

She bit her lower lip. "It was so sudden. I . . . I always thought there was time."

"I lost my father suddenly earlier last year," he heard himself saying. Her father had applauded and been proud of her. His father had turned his back on him, and had been the reason Zachary had taken his mother's maiden name. His father hadn't wanted the Albright name "tarnished." As always, Zachary pushed away the hurt, the disappointment that his father had never changed his mind. As Zach's fame had grown, so had his father's biting censure.

Laurel turned to him, their faces inches apart. Her hand covered his. "I'm sorry."

There was compassion in the beautiful black eyes staring back at him. He had been wrong about her being a snob, but he wanted the conversation to stay on her. "Thank you. You father must have been a great man."

She raised her knees, folded her arms across them, and placed her chin on top. "He was always so proud of my sister and me and always in our corner."

"He did what a father was supposed to do," he said fiercely. He and Paige's father had been demanding, critical. The proud moments were treasured because they came so infrequently.

Her gaze snapped to his. There was sympathy in the dark eyes staring back at him. In trying to comfort her, he had exposed too much of himself. He never did that. Never.

"Thank you for reminding me how lucky I was." She hadn't offered him words of comfort this time, but they were there in her dark, expressive eyes. He briefly wondered how she'd managed to remain so unspoiled in the dog-eat-dog music industry, then immediately thought of the mother who usually traveled with her, and of her father.

"You would have remembered yourself eventually." His fingers slid down her chin. She had incredible skin. It felt like warm silk. He clenched his fist to keep from curving his hand around her neck and bringing her waiting mouth to his. He'd never wanted a woman this fast, this deeply.

He rose to his feet and extended his hand to her. "It's late. I'll see you home."

After a moment's hesitation, she placed her hand in his and stood. He felt her pulse quicken, knew his had done the same. "I can find my way back," she said, her voice a bit breathless.

"I'm a southern boy, born and bred. My mother would disown me." Picking up his jacket, he lightly grasped her arm and started back the way they had come. "I have a Jeep. I can drive you."

"All right." The shadows were no longer in her eyes.

"This way." He steered her to the parking lot adjacent to the restaurant and assisted her into the Jeep, then went around to the driver's side and got in. He looked over at her as she buckled her seat belt.

She glanced up to find her watching her. She went still. "What?"

"Your hair. The top is down."

She chuckled, a soft, alluring sound that went straight to his gut. Her hand lifted, her slim fingers treaded through the thick black strands that fell in wavy profusion to the middle of her back. He wished he could do that for her. "It'll be fine."

Zach started the Jeep and pulled out of the parking space. Her hair might be, but he wasn't so sure about himself. Laurel Raineau drew him in as no other woman ever had before.

"Take a left at the next intersection," she instructed. "My place is at the end of the street. I wanted to take the water taxi over, but there wasn't room."

"Water taxi?" Zachary said, turning onto her street.

"The inner homes and condos of the Navarone Resort are connected by a waterway with a taxi boating service," she explained as he pulled up in front of her door. "Reminds me a bit of Venice."

He switched off the motor. "You travel a lot?"

"Too much." Unbuckling her seat belt, she climbed out and started for the front door of the brightly colored condos in hues of green, red, and orange.

Zach met her at the edge of the sidewalk. Gently grasping her elbow, he walked her to the door, wondering if he should take the opening she presented and ask what she did, then quickly decided against it. If he asked questions, she'd want answers of her own.

"Thank you." Opening her clutch, she took out her key.

"Let me get that." Opening the door, he returned her key. "I've been thinking. I've come here to forget about business and play hooky. If you have no other plans, do you want to play hooky with me?"

She studied him for long moments. He held his breath.

"I don't think I've ever played hooky before," she finally said.

He grinned at the teasing light in her eyes. "Me neither. Which means we can make up the rules as we go. How about I pick you up for breakfast around nine and we can play it by ear from then on?"

"I'd like that. Good night, Zachary."

"My friends call me Zach."

She pushed open the door and turned when she was inside, the teasing smile reappearing on her incredible kissable lips. "Good night." She waited a beat. "Zach."

The door closed. Zach didn't realize he was grinning until he was halfway to his Jeep. He stopped, glanced back at the closed door, the lights illuminating the windows in front of the house.

"Don't even think about getting involved. She's business." Blowing out a breath, he continued to the Jeep, wondering if his brain was listening. His hungry body certainly wasn't.

Three

Laurel resisted the urge to peek through the sheer curtain for one last glimpse of Zach. The man was gorgeous. And they were going to play hooky together. Eight more days at the resort suddenly didn't seem all that bad after all.

Smiling, she turned off the light in the front room and went to the bedroom and straight to her closet. Viewing the colorful assortment of clothes, she was suddenly grateful that Sabra had overruled her and insisted they go shopping to update her wardrobe.

She had dozens of gowns for onstage performances, but except for shoes, her personal wardrobe was pitifully lacking. She wasn't into clothes the way Sabra was. Besides, with her grueling schedule, she had no time to do anything besides perform and rehearse. She never had the chance to visit the famous sights of the cities she played or just relax. Often she didn't even know where she was.

Softly humming to herself, she pulled out a linen-and-silk turquoise ruffled halter that draped just below the waist, and the coordinating white pants with turquoise stitching in the seams and hem. She had the perfect pair of low-heeled turquoise heels to wear. Tomorrow was going to be very interesting, and she couldn't wait.

Zach's cell phone rang just as he opened the door to his cottage on the Navarone estate. He pulled it from the inside of his coat pocket. "Hi, Sunshine."

"Hi. How did the talk with Laurel go?"

Zach stopped in midstride in the front room, worry creeping though him. "Kyle is fast."

"I told Shane it was important to you to talk with her, and since you're important to me, he wanted me to know that you two had connected," she told him. "So?"

"We're having breakfast in the morning. Don't worry," he said, hating that he couldn't be completely honest with her.

"Wonderful," she said. "I knew you'd convince her. There's nothing you can't do when you set your mind to it."

Paige had always been proud of him. He hoped that, when this was over, she would continue to be. "I admire her music and, after meeting her, I admire her as well. We're going to get to know each other."

"Good idea. And you don't need me or anyone else watching over your shoulder. I'll tell Shane as much," Paige told him. "Have fun. We'll talk when you get back. 'Night, Zach."

" 'Night, Sunshine." Zach plopped down on the sofa. He wasn't very pleased with himself. He didn't like lies. He'd always been straightforward and up-front with people, but he hadn't been with Laurel or Paige. This could blow up in his face if he wasn't careful.

His only consolation, if there was one, was that he wasn't doing this for profit or to hurt anyone. Laurel was a gifted violinist. He believed—he knew—he could transfer her onstage magnetism to the CD. Subsequently, she'd sell more CDs, widen her audience, and make a butt-load of money.

Getting up, he ignored the small voice that whispered his nobility might be more believable if seeking his father's approval wasn't in the equation.

"You're beautiful."

Laurel felt a quick rush of pleasure at the open appreciation in Zach's intense black eyes the next morning. "Thank you." He looked get-you-into-trouble gorgeous in navy slacks and a white knit polo shirt that hugged his lean, muscular chest.

Stepping over the threshold of her condo, she closed and locked her front door, then dropped the key into one of the zipper pockets of her oversized beach bag.

"You sleep all right?" he asked.

"Like a log." Unlike the night before when she had tossed and turned, and finally resorted to watching TV. She stopped when they were almost near the sidewalk. "Where's your Jeep?"

He smiled down at her, causing her heart to start tap dancing again. "At the restaurant where we're having breakfast. I thought we'd start off our adventure with something on your list."

From beneath the brim of her woven straw hat with turquoise ribbon around the brim, she stared up into the twinkle in his incredible eyes. There was only one thing she had mentioned, and it had been casual. "You can't mean the water taxi?"

"The driver is waiting for us." Zach led her down a paved walkway just off the street.

She didn't have to think long to realize that people might jump to do things for Laurel Raineau, the concert violinist, but plain old vacationing Laurel Raineau was another matter entirely. It felt good to be treated a bit special when the other person had no ulterior motive.

Laurel spotted the speedboat and driver a short distance down the incline, and grinned. "Thank you."

"I wanted the day to start out fun." Opening the three-foot iron gate leading to the docked boat, Zach ushered her though and down to the pier. *"Buenos días, señorita,"* the young driver greeted her.

"Buenos días," Laurel returned. Taking her seat, she removed her hat and placed her sunglasses on the brim.

"Thanks for waiting." Zachary sat down beside her. "Back to the main landing, please."

"*Sí, señor.*"

Zach smiled down at her. "Still think it's like Venice?"

"Better," she said before she thought and fought not to blush. In Venice the ride had been strictly business. With Zach's warmth seeping into her skin from his muscled thighs against hers to the arm draped lightly around her shoulders, she felt almost wicked, and struggled not to lean closer.

"Good." He reached under the seat, pulled out several pamphlets, and handed them to her. "I picked these up this morning. I thought after breakfast we might stroll the city streets. Then afterward we could go to the main Mayan ruin, or we can go later and stay for the fireworks at night. Depending on when you want to go. On returning, we can have a late dinner and, if you're not tired, dancing."

All of it sounded fun. She grinned up at him. "You're sure you've never played hooky before?"

"Nope, and I'm glad I waited to play with you," he said, his voice a velvet purr.

Her stomach felt all mushy and tight—which didn't make sense. Somehow her gaze drifted to his mouth, probably because he was looking at hers. Her breath trembled out over her lips in uncertain anticipation of his mouth on hers.

"Laurel."

She couldn't say anything. The universe narrowed down to his mouth beckoning hers. Suddenly he turned away. Disappointment and embarrassment hit her.

"We're about to dock," Zach said, his voice strained and hoarse.

She looked up and saw that he was right. Two couples waited to get on. If he hadn't stopped— Her hands unsteady, she put on her hat, donned her shades with an unsteady hand, and placed the brochures in her bag.

"*Gracias,*" Zach said, and helped Laurel out of the boat. She came to the middle of his chest. He could lift her with one arm, yet she made him weak and horny. He stared down at the top of her ridiculous cute hat and wanted to drag her to him, kiss the embarrassment off her face, and replace it with need.

Zach blew out a frustrated breath. "The restaurant is this way." She nodded, her grip on her bag tightening. Something squeezed in his chest. He wanted the playful ready-for-an-adventure Laurel back.

He guided her behind a huge palm tree, then lifted her chin with the tips of his fingers. Her eyes were closed behind her shades. He muttered a curse. She flinched. He removed the glasses. "Please look at me. Please."

Her eyelids fluttered open. Embarrassment stared up at him.

"Please forgive my bad manners. I want today to be fun for you. If I get out of line and try to kiss you again, you have my permission—not that you need it—to punch me."

Her gaze flickered away, then back to him. She licked her lips. His body tightened. "What if I don't want to punch you?"

Zach's entire body clenched with hunger, protectiveness, and a strange kind of gentleness that he had never felt before. He pulled her into his arms, felt the shiver that raced though her body, then her arms going around his waist as she placed her head on his chest.

Lord, what was he going to do? His desire for Laurel had blindsided him. He imagined the same thing had happened to her. Nowhere was there a hint of gossip about her. Her image was unblemished. She'd dated a has-been vocalist for a couple of months about a year ago, but no one had been surprised when things broke off. Sean Conner wasn't in her league.

Zach closed his eyes and held her tighter. Neither was he.

He eased her away from him. She looked up at him curiously, as if she didn't know what to expect. That made two of them. "I didn't foresee this," he told her honestly. At least in that he could be truthful.

"Neither did I."

His hands tenderly cupped her face. There was no deception, no guile in the beautiful brown eyes staring up at him. She was a rarity in their business. "I wonder if you realize how special and unique you are?"

She blinked, then smiled, the tension leaving her body. "Wait until you get to know me better, and then tell me that again."

"I plan to." He kissed her lightly on the lips because he just had to taste her, if only once. "Breakfast." He curved his arm around her waist and started for the restaurant.

"I'm starved," she said, her arm casually going around his waist.

A picture flashed through his usually disciplined mind of her feasting on him instead of food, her hot mouth on his skin as she rubbed her silken body across him, giving him pleasure, driving him crazy with wanting her. He groaned inwardly. It was going to be a very long day.

The city of Playa del Carmen offered something for everyone. There was endless shopping, incredible restaurants, fun on and beneath the Caribbean Sea with all kinds of water sports, but most of all there were the colorful sights and sounds of the unique city that had once been a sleepy fisherman's village on the way to someplace else.

Laurel breathed in the morning air as she and Zach strolled along La Quinta Avenida, stopping occasionally to stare into one of the many shops that ran the gamut from small alcoves offering beautiful arts and crafts handmade by regional artisans to fabulous boutiques that featured designer names.

"We've been doing this almost an hour and you haven't wanted to go inside a single shop or talk to a street vendor about buying anything." He shook his head at her. "See, unique. Just like I said."

She smiled up at him because she couldn't help it. "I'm not much of a shopper. Sa— my sister and mother would be in shopper's heaven." She glanced away, hoping he hadn't caught her slip. Sabra had too unusual a name and was too popular an actress to take a chance. She wanted to remain just a tourist.

"My mother and sister would be right there with them," he joked. "With that said, I probably should buy them something."

"Same here." She paused in front of a jewelry shop. The sterling pieces with turquoise and other stones were exquisite.

"You see something you like?" he asked.

She heard the expectation in his voice and looked up at him. He couldn't possibly be thinking of buying her anything? "My mother and sister love jewelry. Do you mind if we go in?"

He opened the door and reached for her tote. "My sister and mother like their hands free."

"You won't be embarrassed?"

"The bag."

What had she been thinking? He was too self-assured to be embarrassed. And women would still take a second and a third look. One bold woman at the restaurant where they had breakfast couldn't take her eyes off him as she kept whispering something to the woman sitting with her. They both looked to be in their early twenties.

Handing him the tote, she entered the shop.

"*Buenos días, señor y señorita,*" the salesclerk greeted them. "Would you like my assistance or do you wish to look around?"

"Browse, please," Laurel answered.

"Please let me know if there is anything in the case or window you'd like to see," the woman said, then moved away.

"This would go with what you have on and it looks like it might suit you," Zachary said, pointing to a hammered sterling-silver cuff bracelet with a large turquoise center stone.

It was gorgeous, and tempting. Laurel couldn't decide if the piece appealed to her because Zach thought it suited her or because she agreed with him. The only jewelry she wore off stage was a watch given to her by her parents on her sixteenth birthday.

She'd pestered them for months about the TAG diamond bezel watch with diamond markers and the cool blue mother-of-pearl facing. One thing Sabra hadn't been able to do was talk her into buying jewelry that she'd probably never wear.

"There are earrings to match." His finger traced the outline of the chandelier earrings.

Laurel shivered and imagined herself wearing

them, his fingers doing to same thing, then touching her bare skin, lifting her mouth to his. She turned firmly away. "I usually don't wear jewelry."

"You certainly don't need it," he said matter-of-factly.

She swung back around. "What?"

"Jewelry is usually worn to enhance. You don't need it. You're stunning enough the way you are," he said, his voice dropping with each word until he finished in an intimate whisper.

Laurel felt her heart melt. Zach was lethal and endearing. She hadn't known a man could be both.

"Still browsing?" the clerk asked.

Caught daydreaming about Zach, Laurel felt her cheeks heat. "There are a couple of pieces in the window I wanted to see. I'll show you." Laurel moved away, and the woman followed.

Zach motioned to another salesperson as soon as Laurel was busy with the first clerk. Putting his hands to his lips, he pointed to the jewelry pieces he knew would look stunning on Laurel. Giving the clerk his card, he promised to be back later to pick them up.

As he'd said, Laurel didn't need jewelry, but she'd look fantastic wearing the pieces. He didn't doubt he'd have a difficult time getting her to accept the jewelry, but he'd find a way.

He frowned. Carmen was the last woman he'd purchased jewelry for. At the time, her lack of faith in him had hurt as much as her lack of love. With Laurel, it wasn't anything romantic. He'd give her the bracelet and earrings as a way to apologize for not telling her who he was.

Imagining the turquoise pieces on Laurel, he turned and wanted to curse. The young woman from the restaurant came through the door. He didn't know if she had followed him or if she'd seen him though the window. Either way, she was trouble.

An interested woman might have been bold enough to stare, and that would have been the end of it. A fan was relentless. He recognized the glazed look on her face and that of the woman with her. Both were in their early twenties and wore short shorts and halter tops.

He didn't wait for one of them to scream his name or make a scene. Quickly he pulled his agent's card he carried for persistent entertainers who wouldn't take no for an answer from his wallet and went to her. "E-mail him next week and you'll have every album I've ever produced autographed by the artist—if you'll leave now."

She clutched the card, gulped, and stared at him with rapt fascination. The woman with her stared with her mouth gaped. "I-I want an autographed picture of you with my name on it."

He nodded abruptly. "Please leave."

"I—"

"One more word, and you get nothing." Not wanting Laurel to catch him talking to the woman, he walked away. He wasn't fast enough. Laurel looked up at him and then at the woman.

"Have you decided?" he asked, praying the woman would realize that was as good as she was going to get and leave.

Laurel stepped around him and stared, then shook her head. Zach didn't know if it was in disbelief that the woman had followed them, or as a way to warn her off. Despite his best intention, he liked to think it was the latter.

Curving his arm around her shoulder, he turned her back to the jewelry. "If you can't decide what to buy, we'll keep looking. We can go to the ruins anytime."

Laurel gave her attention to the jewelry pieces, then reached for the bag he held. "I'll take those two necklaces. Can you please gift-wrap them?"

"Certainly, *señorita.*"

She handed the salesclerk her credit card and faced him. "I think I'd like to go to the ruins today."

Please, he thought, *let there be no more fans today.* He usually didn't mind because they were the reason he was successful, but the situation with Laurel was too tenuous.

"Then ruins it is. Although it pains me to say so, you'll need to stop back by your place and pick up something to cover your arms, and change shoes."

She lifted her foot, twisted her thong platform wedge sandal. "I guess keeping these on is not worth a sprained ankle."

"No. The sun is going to be brutal later on, and I don't know how much we'll be exposed to it during the tour. Your skin looks delicate." It certainly felt that way, smooth and silky.

She blushed. "What about you?"

"Me?" Few people besides Paige and his mother worried about him when it wasn't related to the music business. "My skin is a lot tougher than yours."

She adamantly shook her head. "If I change clothes, so do you."

Too bad we can't change together, but then if we did, we'd never make it to the ruins. "I'll change."

The Mayan ruins were as beautiful and as haunting and mystical as Laurel had imagined. The site was an impressive reminder of the unique Mayan civilization, their extraordinary accomplishments, and their brilliant mathematical minds. Mysteries still surrounded the sacred temples and the many gods for which they were named.

The most compelling thing about the tour for Laurel, however, was being with Zach. He excited her, made her feel sexy every time his hot gaze touched her—which was often.

On the drive back they'd stopped for dinner and made plans to go dancing later. At her place, she showered and, silently thanking Sabra, put on a black one-shoulder dress with a silver buckle. When she opened the door, Zach simply stared at her for a few moments, his eyes sliding over her. She felt sexy and desirable.

"You're beautiful," he said, the words hushed.

"Thank you."

Taking her arm, he walked her to the Jeep. Tonight the top was up. Getting inside, the skirt of her dress slid up over her knees.

"I like that dress even more," Zach said, with a teasing grin before closing her door. Climbing inside, he drove them into town and parked. "It will be easier if we walk. It's only a short distance."

"All right." She didn't mind walking because she'd be closer to Zach.

"The first night I saw you, I thought moonlight suited you. I still do," Zach said as they strolled down La Quinta Avenida toward the nightclub. The avenue, crowded with people, was lined with bars, restaurants, and exclusive boutiques.

She swallowed. *Thank you* didn't seem the right thing to say.

He turned and guided her up three steps to a recessed doorway. A male attendant opened the door. A pounding beat greeted them. Laurel almost winced. She'd never liked loud music, even as a teenager. Rap set her teeth on edge. Zach's arm tightened a fraction as if he felt her distress.

"Zach Albright," he said to the first waitress he saw.

The woman's eyes widened, then ran quickly over him. "Certainly, Mr. Albright. I'll show you to your private table."

They followed the waitress through the crowded dance club, then up a short flight of stairs to an empty table on a platform with two booths and three other tables. All were occupied. The music was fast and loud, the dance floor packed with gyrating bodies. It wasn't the type of place she would have chosen.

"Not what you're used to?" he asked, his hand in the small of her back, his lips near her ear so she could hear. The warmth of his breath fanned her ear, caused a shiver to race through her.

She shook her head. "I like my music a bit more restrained."

"Your table, Mr. Albright," the waitress said.

"Thank you." Zach pulled out a chair at the small table. "What would you like to drink, Laurel?"

"White wine."

"Two white wines." Zachary took the seat next to hers. "What kind of music do you like?"

"Classical," she answered slowly.

"Your wine." The waitress placed the glasses on the table. "Would you like for me to start a tab?"

"No, thank you." He placed cash on the table.

The woman picked up the money. "I'll check on you in a bit."

"We can go if you're uncomfortable," he said to Laurel as the waitress moved away.

"I'm not uncomfortable." She glanced around. Everyone seemed to be having a great time, even those not on the floor. Their heads and bodies bobbed to the booming rap song. "It's just . . ."

"Loud?"

"Very."

He came to his feet. "Let's go. We'll go for a walk."

She didn't move. All day they'd done what she wanted. She lifted her foot, wiggled the toe of her red-soled peep-toe platform shoe with a four-and-a-half-inch heel. "Don't you think I should get one dance?"

"You're sure?"

She came to her feet. With her heels, if she lifted her head, she could almost brush her lips across his chin. A tempting possibility and one she definitely planned to act upon before the night was over. She flushed. She had to stop thinking about kissing Zach.

His eyes never leaving hers, Zach curved his arm around her waist, drawing her slowly to him. "Let's put those shoes to the test."

By the time they reached the dance floor, the music had changed to a Latin beat. Excited shouts erupted as couples crowded the dance floor. Their movements became fast and sexually charged.

A grin tugged the corner of Zach's incredible mouth. "You game?"

She studied him. He didn't appear the least bit intimidated. She felt a wild exhilaration. She rather liked the idea of tempting him, having his eyes on her. "I believe you promised me a dance."

His arm tightened around her waist, dragging her flush against his muscled hardness. Heat, sexual in its intensity, poured from him. "I like to think I'm a man of my word."

His body swayed with the music, taking her with him. Then he was spinning her away, the hem of her flared skirt swirling around her legs, then bringing her back into his arms. Her leg wrapped around his. She felt his erection, but before she had a chance to get nervous, he spun her away again.

When she returned, her back was against his front. She went sensuously down to the floor, her hands on either side of his body, before coming back up.

Each encounter of their bodies, each heated stroke, created sexual friction to tantalize and tease. Her breasts brushed against his back as she twisted up, then down, then stepped around in front of him to repeat the motion. He twirled her around until she was back in his arms, her back to him, his arm around her waist.

Each movement excited and beckoned. When the music ended, they were plastered against each other from chest to knees, her arms around his neck, her slightly parted lips inches from his.

Another song started, but neither seemed to notice. Their breathing was harsh in the air.

He wanted and he couldn't have.

Taking a deep breath, Zach dropped his forehead against Laurel's. Thankful that the song was slow and no one paid them any attention, he fought to bring the raging hunger of his body under control.

"I better get you home." Releasing her and stepping back was one of the most difficult things he'd ever done. He led her outside and started for the parking lot a short distance away where he'd left the Jeep.

Unfortunately, the cool air did nothing to wipe out the need clawing at him. They walked back to the Jeep in silence, his thoughts troubled. He'd had the crazy idea to show her that people enjoyed different types of music. He'd reasoned the popular nightspot, with music from old school to rap, would be perfect. All he'd accomplished was to get as hard as a rock.

Seating Laurel in the Jeep, he went around to the driver's side and got in. She was quiet as they drove off. What did he expect? He hadn't been able to hide his blatant desire for her.

Parking in front of her condo, he opened his door, helped her out, felt her tremble. When he messed up, he did it big-time.

At her door, her hand shook as she tried to unlock her door. He took the key from her, unlocked and opened her door. As soon as he returned the key, she started inside.

His hand on her arm stopped her. She tensed. She refused to look at him.

"Laurel." He blew out a frustrated breath. "I've tried to fight it, but I touch you and I want you." His laugh was ragged. "I see you and I want you. Nothing has ever happened to me like this. Please look at me, and tell me you forgive me for embarrassing you."

Slowly her head came up. "You didn't embarrass me."

Desire stared back at him. "Laurel."

He pulled her into his arms, his mouth finding hers. Desire hit him full-force. Lifting her into his arms, he went inside her condo, slamming the door behind them.

Four

His mouth slammed into hers, stealing her breath, scattering her thoughts, and sending need plummeting through her. The fierce intensity shook her. She'd never experienced anything like the pleasure of his touch, the craving for more.

His large hand skimmed over her bare shoulder, the curve of her back, before settling on her hips. His erection, bold and unashamed, pressed against her.

A small part of her sent a warning to her brain, but the growing ache in the center of her body that had begun with their dance was too strong to fight. Her arms tightened around his neck, her leg lifted around his to get some relief. He moved sensuously against her.

What thoughts she had scattered, fractured. Her hands clutched him to her; her hips matched his rhythm.

His head abruptly lifted, and Laurel wanted to drag his mouth back. His eyes, fierce with desire, blazed into hers. "You make me weak. I've never wanted like this."

His words melted her heart. Moisture pooled in her eyes. With her body screaming for the ache to go away, she pulled his head down. She sighed with pleasure as his mouth took hers again. His tongue tangled and danced with hers, feeding the passion between them. She twisted restlessly against him, heard the rasp of the zipper on the side of her dress. He stepped away and tugged the dress over her head.

Before her foggy brain could clear, his mouth returned to hers, drawing her into a vortex of passion once again. His hungry mouth moved to her bare shoulder then downward. Her body buckled as his wet, hot mouth closed around her taut nipple, causing the growing ache to deepen.

A moan vibrated through her as his tongue swirled and laved, sending heat sizzling through her body before he moved to the other breast. She arched into him, wanting him more than she'd ever desired a man before. Heat pooled between her thighs.

"Laurel."

The room tilted as he picked her up, his mouth finding her again. She moaned as pleasure swept through her. She felt the cool sheet beneath her back and the heat of his muscled body over hers.

He kissed her as if he had all the time in the world, long, slow, seductive, throwing her off balance again. Her skin felt tight, overly sensitive, his shirt an irritant. She wanted it gone and fumbled with the buttons.

Tearing his mouth away, he pulled the shirt

over his head and kicked free of his pants. Moonlight poured through the large plate-glass window in the bedroom. She had an impression of leashed power before he was crouched over her again.

"You're all that I desire." His mouth skimmed over hers, leaving need and heat in his wake as his lips tantalized and teased. Her body quivered, her heart raced, her breath stuttered. She felt compelled to touch him as he was touching her.

Her hands ran over the muscular warmth of his chest, boldly followed the path with her lips. Air hissed through his teeth.

He muttered her name. She sighed his.

His hand glided lazily over her stomach, the inside of her thigh, increasing the restless edge growing in her. Her legs closed automatically, trapping his hand. His hand flexed, moved, flicked the hidden nub, stroking her. Shock and pleasure had her gasping. Opening her legs, she clutched his shoulders and twisted restlessly beneath him.

"Soon."

She barely noticed the black lace panties being pulled down her legs. He was doing delicious, wild things to her. Her moan turned into a whimper as he increased the pace of his fingers, the pressure. Her head thrashed on the pillow, unfamiliar with the sensations moving through her. She burned.

Quickly sheathing himself, he reared over her, lifting her hips. He wanted this woman. He'd never wanted anything more. It had taken all of his control not to tear off their clothes and take her standing up.

He hadn't because it had been more important to make their first time together unforgettable. Now, staring down at her beautiful flushed face, her heaving breasts, lush and full, her eyes glazed with desire, her silken flesh hot and sensitive, it had been worth every nerve-racking second. The wait was finally over.

He plunged into her moist heat, felt the slight resistance. Her surprised gasp mixed with his own. Even as his mind rebelled, she frantically tried to push him away.

The distress tore at his heart. He reacted instinctively to soothe, to bring back the passion that had led him to believe that she was experienced. Keeping his body still, he kissed her, sweet and light, luring her back to him.

After a scary moment, her tongue tentatively met his. Weak with relief and thankfulness that she still wanted him, his hands lovingly stroked her. Her body softened. Grateful, he reached between them and flicked his thumb across the sensitive nub, found her center wet. He deepened the kiss.

She met him, kiss for kiss. Her hips lifting, seeking. He removed his hand and began to move slowly, letting her body adjust to his. He increased the pace by degrees, finding her with him, matching his rhythm, her breathing as off kilter as his own.

"My joy," he murmured, his control slipping away. His body plunged in and out of hers, taking them over at the same time. When he had the strength, he rolled to his side, bringing her with him and tucking her against his length.

Questions swirled around in his head. He'd been the first. The knowledge made his chest tight and his heart beat faster. He'd never been a possessive man, but he accepted that he was with her. Angling his head, he stared down at her. She was asleep. No wonder. They'd been out most of the day. To his way of thinking, it had ended perfectly.

His eyes abruptly shut. He groaned. He shouldn't have touched her. In the past, he had never had any difficulty walking away. With her, the sweet hunger overwhelmed him. Their shared passion was a starting point. He'd make this right.

He had to. The alternative wasn't acceptable.

Laurel slowly woke with a smile on her face, stretched, felt the slight soreness where she'd never felt it before. She frowned, felt the warmth of Zach's body curved against her back, his hand lightly splayed on her bare abdomen. The night came crashing back.

What had she done? She shut her eyes. Stupid question. Shame and misery hit her, knotting her stomach. She'd never acted so irresponsibly. Yet even as her thoughts jumbled, her body hummed, wanted his. She had to get out of there.

She made a motion to sit up. The arm curved around her waist suddenly tightened.

"No." The one word, was flat, inflexible.

She shut her eyes. "Please."

"If I let you go, I might never see you again."

That was exactly what she wanted. *Liar.* Already her blood rushed hotly through her veins. She felt his arousal against her back and wanted to press her hips against him, roll over on her back and . . . She groaned.

"Honey, please listen. Neither one of us expected this to happen. You waited for a reason." His cheek rested against her hair. "If you have to blame someone, blame me."

She shook her head. Honesty dictated she share the responsibility. She had acted as if she knew what she was doing. She vividly recalled pressing against him, attempting to take off his shirt. "I'm responsible for my own actions."

His hand tenderly stroked up and down her arm. "It's no excuse, but I've never lost control like that."

"Me, either," she whispered.

His hand cupped her chin, turned her face toward him. "Last night was unbelievable. Holding you in my arms, hearing you call my name is probably as close to heaven as I'll ever get."

Some of the tension seeped out of her. She finally understood what all the hoopla was about sex. It was explosive and mind blowing. It could take you under its seductive spell from one heartbeat to the next.

"I'm going to my place, shower, and then come back. Where I'm staying is isolated with a private beachfront. We can spend the day swimming or just doing nothing."

She simply shook her head.

"Yes. You have nothing to be ashamed of. I hope you aren't sorry," he said, worry creeping into his voice.

"It shouldn't have happened."

"Are you sorry?"

She should be, and that made her even more confused. She glanced away.

"I won't press you for an answer, but you aren't going to beat up on yourself." Kissing her bare shoulder, he pulled up the sheet to cover her back and rolled away. "I'll be back in thirty minutes. There's a small kitchen where I'm staying. On the way over there, we can stop and pick up some food."

Laurel said nothing. The moment he left, she was leaving. She'd get a room at a hotel if necessary, until she could get a flight out.

Zach walked into her line of vision and knelt. He had his pants on, but his shirt was unbuttoned. Laurel averted her eyes. She recalled too vividly kissing his broad chest, running her hands over the muscled warmth. She wanted to again.

"If you run, I'll follow you," he said, his voice unyielding. "Just because it happened quickly doesn't mean it isn't right." He reached out and gently brushed her hair behind her ear. "I'd like nothing better than for us to stay in bed and make love all day. Maybe tomorrow." Kissing her lightly on the forehead, he came to his feet. "Last night wasn't a vacation fling. The only way I can prove that to you is if you stay."

Laurel heard the front door close. She sat up in bed, drew the sheet over her naked breasts, and put her forehead in the palm of her hand. She should be calling for a taxi to take her to a hotel instead of just sitting there. The reason was simple: She wanted to believe Zach.

If she left, she'd never learn if he was telling the truth. She didn't know anything about him. He appeared successful, but that didn't mean he was. Still, he'd never even hinted that he wanted her to pay for anything.

What did she know about Zachary Albright? Nothing, except he was the most gorgeous man she'd ever met, kissed like a dream, and made her body crave his touch. He was also attentive, kind, thoughtful.

She massaged her temples and then glanced at the phone. She hadn't seen Kyle yesterday and could only hope that, once he'd seen her with Zach, he'd gone about his business. Rio had given her a phone number to call if she had any problems. If she called him, he'd find out about Zach, but Rio might want to know the reason.

She had absolutely no idea what to do and no one to ask for advice. Ashamed of the way she'd behaved, she couldn't call Sabra.

The doorbell made her jump. *Zach.* She wasn't

ready to see him again. The doorbell rang again, then there was knocking.

"Delivery for *Señorita* Raineau," an accented Spanish voice called.

Frowning, Laurel put on a thick terry-cloth robe and went to the front door. "Yes?"

"Delivery for *Señorita* Raineau."

She reached to open the door, then went to the window and looked out. A man stood there with a large bouquet. She opened the door. "I'm Ms. Raineau."

The man smiled and handed her an armful of fresh yellow roses, daisies, and lilies.

"Where do I sign?" she asked.

"No signature, *señorita*." Smiling broadly, he went back to a flower cart, looked at his watch, and leaned against the side.

Laurel closed the door. A piece of paper torn from a small spiral notepad was stuck in the flowers. She pulled it out.

Please stay. Zach.

Laurel plopped down on a chair. He wasn't making this easy for her. Which was probably exactly what he planned. She wasn't a spontaneous person. She thought things through—which had saved her from being used by Sean. She'd been flattered by his attention, the two dozen roses that arrived almost daily for the two months they'd dated.

She glanced down at the cut flowers in her hand and treasured them more. Lifting them to her nose, she smelled the sweet fragrance. She'd been attracted to Zach from the first moment she saw him smiling down at her.

The doorbell rang again. She came to her feet, sure it was Zach this time. She opened the door and saw the same deliveryman with another bouquet of flowers. He handed it to her and started back to his cart. Laurel stood, waiting to see if he left. He didn't. Closing the door with an unsteady hand, she pulled out another piece of notebook paper and read the note.

Please stay. Zach.

"Oh, Zach," she murmured and started back to her bedroom.

Zachary quickly showered and dressed, then jumped in the Jeep and drove straight to Laurel's condo. He could only hope the street vendor had been able to detain her. He didn't want to give her time to leave. He wanted her to know last night had been important to him.

He cared about her. It surprised him how much. While watching her sleep in his arms, he'd never felt such contentment or so blessed. If he wasn't scared of losing her, he would have told her the truth about his identity once they left the nightclub.

His hands flexed on the steering wheel. He had to show her how much she meant to him. It was the only way out of the mess he'd made. He hadn't planned on making love to her, but he was caught up in a desire that, once unleashed, was difficult to control.

His heart thundered when he didn't see the vendor's cart. He braked sharply and hurried to the front door. "Laurel! Laurel!" He banged on the door, and when there was no answer, he hurried toward his Jeep. He'd check every hotel in the area if he had to.

"Zach."

He turned. Laurel stood in the doorway. He didn't stop until she was in his arms, his lips on hers. He felt the fire zip through him, his control slipping again, and pulled back. "I thought you'd left me." He hadn't meant the words to come out so desperate, but he couldn't have cared less.

Laurel was still here. He hadn't lost her. Gently guiding her back inside, he closed the front door.

"I couldn't." She bit her lower lip. He hungered to do that for her. "Thank you for the flowers, but don't you think you overdid it a bit."

He pulled her to him again. "I saw him on my way to change. You're too well mannered not to accept a delivery. I told him to keep delivering flowers every five minutes or so until I got back. I guess I panicked when I didn't see his cart."

"I figured you must have told him something like that, so I asked how many more notes he had. When he told me three, I took them and the three bouquets so I could bathe in peace."

"Sorry."

He didn't look sorry. "I love flowers."

"That's what I was counting on." He grabbed her hand and took her to the door of her bedroom. "Grab a swimsuit, sundress, sandals. If you get tired of my cooking we can go out to eat. Our first stop is the market. I'm starved and you must be, too."

"We might stay that way. I can't cook," she said, wrinkling her pretty nose.

He kissed her. He couldn't help it. He still had time. "I didn't expect you to. Today I take care of you."

"Please don't be a lie," she whispered.

Zach's heart clenched painfully in his chest. His arms closed around her, his mouth taking her. There was desperation coupled with hunger as his tongue tangled with hers, lapping at the sweetness, telling her in the only way he could that what he felt for her was genuine. Reluctantly he lifted his head. Trembling hands framed her face. "Believe that. Believe me."

Her smile was tremulous, but it was there. "If you can't cook, you're going to be in so much trouble."

The vise around his chest eased. "I'll let you be the judge. Go get your things so we can get out of here."

Sliding her arms from around his neck, Laurel went to her bedroom. Zach shoved his hand through his hair. Somehow he'd make things right. He had to. Just the thought of her not being in his life made his gut twist painfully.

"Ready." She returned wearing a sexy strapless sundress that stopped just above the incredible knees he fondly recalled kissing. In her hand she carried a large tote, a wide-brimmed straw hat, and a purse. On her feet were barely there, three-inch high-heeled sandals. She looked fantastic.

"Then let's get out of here." Zach ushered her out of the house, locking the door after them.

Laurel was amazed by Zach's knowledge of foods and his ability to haggle with the vendors. He seemed to enjoy it as much as they did. In less than thirty minutes they had several bags and were back in the Jeep, heading to his cottage. Around the third or fourth bouquet of flowers she'd decided to trust her heart, trust Zach.

"We're almost there." The Jeep broke through a clearing.

Ahead was a dazzling white two-story home. Several towering palm trees were in the yard. On the veranda, huge baskets of ferns mixed with trailing red flowers twirled in the morning breeze. The house looked cool and inviting against the dense green foliage on either side and behind it. "A friend of my sister owns the home. My cottage is in back."

"It's beautiful here," she said as Zach pulled to a stop. Getting out, she grabbed a plastic bag in each hand.

He grabbed the other bags and stopped in front of her. "I suppose you're going to be stubborn again and not let me carry those."

"It's the least I can do since I can't cook. Stop stalling. I'm starving here."

He kissed her on the cheek. "Come on then. It's a short distance away."

Laurel started after Zach on the stone path around the side of the house, noting again the dense native trees and shrubs. Then she found something much more interesting to look at: Zach's butt. She bit her lips to keep from laughing. The man was built with defined muscles and an easy strength that still made her breath catch when she thought about it.

"What do you think?"

Her gaze jerked up. It took her a few moments to realize he was talking about the cottage. It was white with a vine-covered pergola that formed a room-like courtyard. Whoever the owner was, he had created a restful retreat. "It's charming."

"I usually like a lot of space, but the place has grown on me. Come on." Bounding up the three steps, he opened the door.

Laurel frowned and followed. "You didn't lock it?"

A strange expression crossed his face. "The owner has security on site while he's away, so it's safe."

She stepped inside and was immediately captivated. Soft hues of blue and yellow dominated the airy front room. The floors were opaquely stained ash hardwood. The furnishings were simple antiques and down-filled upholstery furniture, giving the area a soothing open feeling. "I see what you mean. It's wonderful."

"The kitchen is this way." He went to an adjoining room off the living room. "I'll have your breakfast in no time. Omelet and fried potatoes with onions all right?"

"I'm from Nashville, so it couldn't be better." She placed her bags on the stainless-steel counter and began removing items, hoping Zach would want to share a little of his background as well.

He took a large bowl from beneath the cabinet. "I grew up in Atlanta. I guess you could say we were privileged, but my mother was always down-to-earth, just like her parents."

Laurel placed the eggs and vegetables on the counter. "Did your mother teach you how to cook?"

He smiled, then washed and peeled the potatoes. "She said she didn't want me starving when I went away to college. Besides, when I got married, I could help out my wife." His gaze caught the question in her eyes. "Never married. I was serious only once, a lifetime ago."

Did she have the right to ask what happened? After last night she did. "What happened?"

"I wasn't what she wanted." He shrugged and reached for a skillet.

Laurel wished she was intuitive enough to know if there was regret in his voice. "What can I do to help?"

"Nothing. Have a seat." He reached for the carton of eggs.

"I should be doing something," she protested. Unrelated to business, no one besides her family had ever taken care of her.

"You are." He turned to whisk the eggs.

"What?"

He tossed a look over his shoulder that melted her heart and heated her blood. "Making every breath I take that much sweeter."

Laurel sank into a chair. "Zach."

His dark eyes narrowed, then he went back to whisking eggs. "Breakfast and then I want to show you something."

"What is it?"

"Something that we're both going to enjoy."

"A hammock?"

Zach grinned and gave the hammock tied between two large palm trees a slight push. "I saw it when we were shopping this morning."

Laurel's gaze moved from him to the blue-and-white-striped hammock. "Will it hold us?"

"I tested it while I had you wait in the house." He gave it another playful shove. "We can see the sea from here and just relax. You game?"

She looked at the knots securing the hammock to the towering palms, then back to him. "You can cook, but . . ."

"I was an Eagle Scout, plus my roommate in college had a home in the Hamptons. We spent a lot of time on his sailboat. These knots won't give." To demonstrate, he lay down, then wiggled, laughing as her eyes widened in alarm, reaching out to catch him in case he started to fall.

Chuckling, she shook her head. "You're like a kid."

He held his arms out to her. "Come on, let me hold you." He wanted that more than anything.

She took a tentative step toward him, slipped out of her heels, eased down on the hammock, and lay back. Her body immediately rolled halfway on top of his. "Sorry."

"I'm not." His arms closed around her. He kissed the top of her head. "I'm still taking care of you."

She sighed, rubbed her cheek against his chest, and snuggled closer. "This is nice."

He set the hammock in motion. "Go to sleep. When you wake up we'll decide what to do—if anything."

She sighed again. "Thank you, Zach."

He kissed the top of her head again and said nothing. With those words, she cut deeply into his heart and left a bitter taste in his mouth. She was thanking the person she thought he was.

He hadn't wanted Laurel hurt, but it was too late now. Even as he held her, he had a feeling that this was going to blow up in his face, and when it did Laurel would be lost to him forever.

Laurel woke up in Zach's arms. This time she knew exactly where she was. Beneath her cheek, his heartbeat accelerated. She lifted her head and stared into his dark eyes swirling with desire. She didn't think. She kissed him, the hammock swaying.

She threw her leg over him, climbing on top to leisurely taste his mouth. His large hands slid up and down her back, finally settling on her hips, holding her against his erection.

Heat, fire, and need churned through her. She was in control and enjoyed every passionate moment. She broke the kiss and stared down at him.

His hand tunneled through her hair, massaged her scalp. "You sleep all right?"

"Yes." She traced his sensual lower lip with her fingertip. "You?"

"I'd rather hold you than sleep."

Her forehead touched his chest. "Zach, you do have a way with words."

His hand lifted her head until her warm breath fluttered across his face. "It's you. You make me want to be better."

She frowned. "You're one of the sweetest, most caring men I've ever met."

His smile wistful, he glanced at his watch. "You have twenty minutes to make it to your appointment at the Tree Spa for the works."

She jerked up, causing the hammock to lurch. "The Tree Spa. I called and they were booked."

He curved his arms around her waist and beneath her knees and stood. Still carrying her in his arms, he started for the house. "I guess they had a cancellation."

"You did more than watch me sleep."

"I never want you to look back on the time we spent together with regret." He went up the steps. Opening the door, he went inside the house.

"You do so much for me," she said, shaking her head as he set her on her feet. "I do nothing for you."

He stared down at her, then lightly kissed her. "Just by being you, you give me more than I thought possible, more than I deserve. Now get your tote or you'll be late."

"I'm going, but I'll surprise you tomorrow." Laurel went to get her bag, planning her surprise for Zach.

The Tree Spa was as wonderful and as posh as she'd heard, and the technicians were skilled. Laurel loved the indulgence of being pampered. She felt rejuvenated, her skin dewy fresh. She smiled to herself on leaving. She couldn't wait for her bare skin to touch Zach's. It amazed her how his hard, muscular body felt so good against her. They fit.

Zach was waiting for her and walked her to the Jeep. Before helping her in, he leaned over and sniffed behind her ear. "You smell and look fantastic."

"I feel the same way." She climbed in and slipped on her hat. "Thank you again. What did you do while I was at the spa?"

"Missed you," he said. Pulling off, he easily maneuvered through the busy streets. "How does grilled shrimp and steak with baked potato sound?"

"You cooked?"

"I figured you'd want to relax and not stand in line for a table." He stopped on the side of the main house and came around the Jeep to help her out, but she was already on the ground.

She bit her lips. It was almost dark. Did he expect her to spend the night? She wasn't sure how she felt about them being intimate again.

"But if you'd rather go out or call it a night, I understand." He fished the keys back out of his pant pocket.

She hooked her arm through his. She trusted Zach. If she wanted to leave after dinner, he'd take her home. "I'm where I want to be."

"Then let's go eat dinner."

"Your mother must be a fantastic cook," Laurel said as she sat on a blanket on the beach beside Zach and watched the setting sun paint the huge sky breathtaking hues of pink and blue.

"She is, but she does everything well," he said casually, his arm draped around Laurel. She'd asked more questions since last night, but he understood the reason. She'd made love with a man she knew very little about. "She still calls and asks if I'm eating well."

"My mother is the same way." Laurel kept her head on Zach's shoulder. "She's attending her fortieth high school reunion. She called while I was at the spa. She's having a ball."

"And probably wondering about you?"

"I told her I was having a fabulous time being pampered and eating too many high-calorie foods."

"Ah."

That one word held a wealth of meaning. "I didn't know how to tell her about you." She sat up and wrapped her arms around her up-drawn knees. "I made love with a man I barely know. I'm sitting here on the beach with him, knowing full well we'll probably end up in bed again tonight."

"Not if you don't want to."

She looked back at him. He was leaning back on his elbows, watching her with a single-minded intensity that made her nipples pucker, her body clench. The lantern he'd brought with them to light their way back to the cottage cast shadows over his strong, determined face. Whatever he did that he had decided to take a break from, Laurel was positive he was successful.

"What brought you to Riviera Maya?"

He was silent so long she didn't think he would answer. The first night he'd said he wanted to forget about business.

"A willful, petulant act of self-indulgence." He sat up, curving his hand around her neck, his breath mingled with hers. "Then I met you, and everything changed."

Her skin prickled with desire. Her clothes felt heavy. For the first time in her life, she felt desirable, felt a woman's power over a man, this man.

Her lips brushed across his, suckled his lower lip. He was so gorgeous. So tender and caring. "I saw you and my heart stopped."

"If I kiss you, I won't stop until I'm buried deep inside you," he said, his voice hushed and strained. "Tell me what you want."

She didn't have to think. "You. In a big comfortable bed."

"Laurel." Her name was a guttural sound of need. Before the sound died, he stood and had her in his arms. Laurel managed to snag the lantern as he started back to the house at a fast clip.

Five

Zach didn't stop until he was beside the bed. Placing Laurel on her feet, he took the lantern from her and put it on the night table, his gaze never leaving hers. "Are you sure?"

She tugged his polo shirt over his head and tossed it onto a nearby chair. "Very."

Zach turned the wick down on the lantern, casting the room in a soft glow, then jerked back the bed covering. Taking her willing body into his arms, he gently, slowly kissed her lips when what he really wanted was to hurry. "You're everything that I desire."

Her small hand trembled on his chest. Her tongue flickered across his nipple, causing air to hiss through his teeth. She gazed up at him with desire shimmering in her eyes. "Then show me."

He intended to do just that. This time there was no doubt that she was with him all the way. His brushed his mouth against hers, a slow, maddening glide that inflamed and teased. She pressed against him, asking for a deeper kiss. When he didn't comply, she curved her hand around his neck, rubbed her breasts against his chest.

Desire shot through him. This time there was nothing tentative about the kiss. He was a man claiming his woman. Each kiss, each brush of their bodies fueled the need for more.

"Bed," he muttered, swinging her up in his arms, and tumbled them into the queen-sized brass bed.

Well aware that with her his control was tenuous, he reached for his belt. She came to her knees and watched his every moment. He grew hard and heavy, his breathing uneven.

Hooking his thumbs over his briefs and pants, he started to slide them down. He stopped as she leaned forward, her breath seeming to catch. *Anticipation.*

Shoving the pants and briefs off, he reached for her. "You looked breathtakingly beautiful today in this dress and all I could think about was taking it off." His finger traced over her skin at the top of the bodice, his eyes narrowed in concentration. "Your skin is like silk." His gaze lifted to hers. "And I want to taste every delectable inch."

Her body clenched painfully, the wanting at a feverish pitch, and all he had done was kiss her, lightly touch her. His name trembled over her lips.

His head lowered. She felt the warmth of his breath, then the heat of his tongue. She moaned, waited for him to pull the bodice down. He didn't. He just continued the maddeningly swirl of his tongue on her skin just above her dress, teasing her.

When she thought she would either scream or put his lips on her aching nipple, he slipped the dress beneath her breasts, kissing every inch of the way as he drew it from her body.

The sweet torture had her twisting beneath him. His tongue dipped into her navel, the action boldly erotic. Her sharp intake of breath was loud in the room. He worshiped her, possessed her, until she quivered with the fierce need to be joined with him again.

Quickly putting on a condom, he came back over her, stared into her eyes, and slowly slid into her hot center. Pleasure unceasing spiraled through her as he filled her. She clenched around him, holding him tight within her body.

Locking their hands together, he began to move, surging into her again and again. Each deep thrust brought them closer to completion, pushed them higher.

With the next breath she arched her hips, spasmed. He was there with her, joining her. She clenched around him, holding him to her until the quakes gradually subsided.

She felt boneless and happy. Her eyes closed, then snapped open as Zach picked her up. "Where are we going?"

"Jacuzzi." He kept walking. "I didn't take you last night because I selfishly wanted to keep holding you."

Her heart sighed as he tucked her in his lap

and ran the water. "You're taking care of me again."

"Always." Kissing her lips, he stepped into the warm, swirling water, still holding her. "Tonight I can do both, hold you and care for you. Close your eyes and relax. I'm here."

With a smile on her face, she did as he asked, feeling cherished, glad that she had remained in Mexico.

The next morning Zach watched Laurel wake up by slow degrees. Her body uncurled in his arms, rubbing sensuously against him, the beautiful smile blossoming on her face that he'd go to his grave remembering. Her nipples brushed against his chest, her leg slid up and down his.

Need and hunger curled through him. He grew heavy, yet he didn't move. Watching Laurel unfold like some exotic flower hidden deep in the jungle was worth the sharp claws of need scraping over him.

Black lashes fluttered against her incredible silky skin. He frowned, his eyes narrowing. He relaxed on seeing that the stubble on his face hadn't marred her skin. He hadn't lied about wanting to take care of her.

But you did lie.

The truth pierced him. It could cost him the woman in his arms. He'd do whatever it took to keep her.

Her eyelids lifted. "Good morning."

Thrusting everything from his mind, he brushed

his lips across hers. "Good morning. You sleep all right?"

She grinned, slow and easy, sliding against him as she moved closer to his face. "Never better."

"Good." He felt her from her soft breasts to her flat stomach to the junction of her thighs. They'd made love twice, then he'd awakened her just before dawn to make love again. His body couldn't get enough.

His hand speared through her tasseled black hair, remembered it splayed on his pillow, wished they were in the wide bed at his LA home. After Carmen, his encounters with women had been fleeting, and not once had he wanted to stick around afterward or take care of one. He never made love at his place.

With Laurel everything changed. He'd have no regrets if . . . He pushed the unwanted thought away. Somehow he'd find a way to explain things to her. "You ready for breakfast?"

She rose up, unself-conscious and so sensually beautiful that his breath caught, his heart thundered. She chuckled and lazily crawled on top of him. "You have a fixation on food."

He brushed the hair out of her face. "You. You're the most beautiful thing I've ever seen. I see you and I want you."

"Sounds like a plan to me." Her mouth brushed across his, bit lightly on his lower lip, then suckled. Her hands weren't idle. One brushed lightly against his cheek; the other trailed leisurely down his stomach to stroke the inside of his thigh.

Breath shuddered harshly over his lips. "You keep that up and breakfast will have to wait."

"This is what you do to me," she whispered as her lips, feather-soft, trailed over his face, the side of his neck. "You shatter my thoughts, make me want things I never imagined, and all of them in your arms."

He sensed she wanted to be in control. He just hoped he was up to it.

She took one of his nipples into her mouth, flicked her tongue across the tip. Groaning, he grabbed a fistful of sheet instead of grabbing her hips and diving into her hot, tight center. She moved to the other nipple and repeated the act.

"Laurel." The sound came out guttural, a plea.

"You taste and smell better than any food." Her mouth moved down his chest, and so did her hand. She cupped him.

His body came off the bed and he grabbed more sheet, wondering how much longer he could withstand the sweet torture. He got his answer when her hand closed around his heavy erection, her thumb flicking across the top as her tongue delved into his navel.

In the next second he twisted and was on top of her. His hands fumbled as he put on a condom. He caught the pleased, satisfied smile on her face seconds before he captured her hips and plunged into her moist sheath. She clamped around him.

"Yes," she murmured, her hands going around his neck.

He measured the length of her, stroking, his hips pumping. Her legs clamped around his waist as he loved her. She shattered in his arms moments later. He followed.

It was a long time before his breathing returned to normal. Aware that if he didn't move, he'd make love to her again, he scooped her up into his arms and headed for the shower. Laurel was a burning hunger that he'd never completely appease. Setting her on her feet, he turned away and adjusted the water.

The moment he faced her, he realized his mistake. She had her arms upraised, trying to braid her hair. The motion lifted her lush, perfect breasts. He hardened and groaned.

Instantly she dropped her arms and placed her hand on his arm, her eyes filled with worry. "What's the matter? Are you all right?"

"Showering together was a bad idea," he said.

A slow smile spread across her incredible face. She reached around him and picked up a bar of soap, lathered her hands, and swept them down his chest. "Depends on how you look at it."

"You aren't the only one who can pull off a great surprise," Laurel said later that morning, walking backward in front of Zach, one hand holding her hat in the gentle breeze.

"Seeing you happy is enough," he said, meaning it. She was such an unexpected delight. To look at her dressed in a white lace sleeveless top over a white tank with white cropped pants, you'd never guess she had pushed him to the edge last night and this morning with her sweet loving.

She stopped and waved her arm toward a sleek sixty-foot sailboat. "Your surprise."

Zach looked from her to the boat, then to the middle-aged burly man in a T-shirt, walking shorts, and deck shoes who was approaching. Laurel's grin widened.

"Good morning, Ms. Raineau. Mr. Albright. I'm Sam Willis. I care for the boat for Mr. Marshall." The man extended his hand to Zach's and held on. "You'll take good care of the *Witch*, won't you?"

"Zach has been sailing for ages," Laurel told the nervous man, hooking her arm through his. "The owner's ship is in good hands."

The man looked pained and handed Zach the keys. "She's ready to go, but I don't mind captaining her for you. I do it all the time for Mr. Marshall when he has guests."

Obviously the man was relinquishing control of the boat under duress. Zach had tried to hire a private boat to take them out, but all of them were booked. Mentioning Blade's name had gotten an appointment to the Tree Spa, which was owned by Navarone Resorts and Spas. Rolling Deep had gained them entrance to the nightclub. He was positive Blade's name had been used again. The sailboat probably belonged to a friend or associate of his.

"You don't have to worry," Laurel assured the man again.

Zach took pity on Willis, who was practically wringing his hands. "Why don't you come aboard and watch me take her out? If you're not satisfied with the way I handle her, I'll turn her over to you."

"I'll get the towline." Willis rushed to untie the boat.

"You're a softy, Zach Albright," Laurel whispered and headed for the gangplank.

Zach followed, a smile on his face.

"So, how did you pull it off?" Zach asked at the helm of the boat. Laurel stood in front of him with her back pressed against his. The wind lightly tossed her hair.

"A friend of the family interceded," she said. "Few, if any people, say no to him."

Blade Navarone. He'd been right. "Why didn't you ask him to get you into the spa?" Zach asked.

"Because this is more important." She grinned up at him.

His chest felt tight. Leaning over, he kissed the top of her head. Her hair danced in the breeze. Each time one of the silken strands touched his skin he remembered it on his body last night and this morning as she had slowly driven him beyond his control. "You constantly amaze me and make me want to be better."

"If we didn't have an audience, I'd kiss you."

Not for the first time, Zach wished he hadn't caved about dropping off the caretaker as planned. But the man had looked so stricken when Zach had mentioning turning back to drop him off, Zach had kept sailing. "A good sailor loves his boat. It's more than just the means of making a living. It's a part of him."

"I feel that way about my vi—"

Zach was glad for the dip of the boat at that very moment. He'd probably tensed as much as Laurel had. If she admitted who she was, he'd have to do the same. He wasn't sure she was ready for that yet, but he couldn't keep putting it off.

"I wanted a guitar when I was twelve. My father was against it so I saved up enough to buy one at a pawnshop. Of course my mother discovered it in my room, but she never said anything. It was our secret," he recalled fondly. "I still have that guitar and wouldn't take anything for it."

"Do you play for a band or something?" she asked cautiously.

He shook his head. "I don't play professionally, but I can do a mean imitation of Jimi Hendrix. That was one gifted man."

"His life was too short," she said, her voice sad. "I wonder if he would have been happier if he'd never hit it big."

"I doubt it. He's another example of his career being who he was," Zach said. "He had so much natural talent. His guitar was an extension of him. Few musicians are gifted, or should I say blessed, with that incredible innate ability. He left us way too early. His legacy is the extraordinary music. No matter what, the work stands. That's all any good musician can ask for, to be proud of the music."

"So you think musicians should never settle for anything less than their best?" she asked a bit cautiously.

"Yes." He wondered if she had doubts about her albums. She gave everything when she played on stage. "Never. They owe it to themselves and their public to do their best every time they walk up to that mike." Zach brought the boat around. He was on dangerous ground, but Laurel's recordings could be so much better and, from her question, she had concerns. "Hendrix put his heart and soul into his playing. He made you feel. His spirit was strong."

Turning, she curved her arm around his waist. "Will you play for me before we leave?"

"Finding a guitar won't be difficult here, but I haven't played in years," he confessed. "You might run screaming from the room with your ears covered."

"I'll take that chance. I can't imagine you not doing anything well."

Something in her voice had him staring down at her. She looked innocent, but he saw the teasing glint in her eyes. He laughed and she laughed with him, the sound carrying on the wind and creating its own music.

"Play." Laurel handed Zach the electric guitar. She'd inquired about a music shop from Willis. He had gladly given them the information and sent them happily on their way and away from the *Witch*. Luckily, a music store was only a few blocks from the dock.

"You're sure?" he asked, holding the guitar by the neck.

"Stop stalling." She was overjoyed that he loved and played a stringed instrument. It made the connection between them even better. There wasn't a violin in the shop or she might have been tempted to play for him. She wanted to. Her fingers actually itched to do so. One day. "Give me your best Hendrix imitation."

Zach tucked the guitar under his arm, strummed a chord, then tightened the strings. His brow lifted. His thick black hair was wind-tossed, and she couldn't wait to get her fingers in it again. "You certainly know how to put on the pressure."

"You're up to it," she said with complete confidence, folding her arms across her chest.

The high-pitched sound caught her off guard. Her hands slowly came to her sides.

Head bent, Zach hit another chord. If her eyes had been closed she would have sworn it was Jimi Hendrix playing "Purple Haze." The music changed to the distinctive staccato of flamenco, then again to a favorite tune of her father, "Brick House" by the Commodores. He'd often teased her mother that the song had been written just for her. The thought brought a smile to her face instead of the usual sadness.

When Zach finished, there was complete silence, then loud applause and screams from the women in the shop.

"*Magnifico,*" said one of the salesclerks, applauding loudly. "*Magnifico.*"

"*Gracias.*" Zach handed the grinning man the instrument, pulled a couple of twenties from his wallet, and gave them to the man.

Zach's gaze flickered around the shop, which had filled with people. If she hadn't known better, Laurel would have thought he looked uneasy. He grabbed her arm. "Let's get out of here."

He moved through the crowd with enviable ease. She didn't know if he was embarrassed or not. She would have liked to have had him play some more, but she didn't like the way the women were reaching out to touch him as he passed as if he were some rock star.

"Girl, I tell you he looks like R.D. before he grew that beard. You know he's my man."

"Only in your dream, Kita. But if it is him, where's his posse?"

"He doesn't need a posse. That's why they call him Rolling Deep."

Laurel stopped and jerked around toward the women talking. Their eyes were glued on Zach.

Firm pressure on her arm kept her moving. Zach didn't slow down until they were a couple of blocks away and the people on the streets had swallowed them up.

"Did you hear who that woman thought you were?" she asked as they continued at a slower pace down the street. "It's a good thing you got us out of there or we might have been mobbed."

"Let's get the Jeep. We can drive to the Mayan ruins and watch the fireworks display."

"He has the worst reputation. No self-respecting real artist would work with him."

"I'll drop you by your place so you can change."

"Rolling Deep." She sneered the name. "He's probably a thug. I wouldn't be surprised if he has a police record."

Zach stopped abruptly. "Have you ever met the man?"

She blinked and stared up into Zach's tight face, his hair tumbled around his shoulders. For a split second he looked dangerous. She almost took a step backward. "No, and I don't want to."

"Have you ever considered that the tabloids sell more papers with titillating lies than printing the truth? That you might be wrong about him?"

She opened her mouth then closed it, shoved her hand through her hair. "I don't care a flying fig about the man. He's not worth discussing or getting upset over."

He stared at her a long time, then took her
arm and started walking again.

She glanced up at him and saw the rigid line
of his jaw. "Are you upset with me?"

He took a few steps before stopping and staring down at her. "I think you've led a sheltered
life."

Her chin hitched. "Is that your way of calling
me narrow-minded just because I don't like music that can cause deafness or a man with a horrible reputation?" He waited a second too long
to answer. "Please take me back to my condo."

"All right."

Laurel got inside the Jeep and slammed the
door. She and Zach had just had their first fight.

Laurel slammed the door to her condo, leaving
Zach standing in the doorway. As soon as the
echo died, she wanted to open the door again
and tell him she was sorry. She shoved her hand
through her hair again.

How had they gotten into an argument over a
man neither of them knew? She turned toward
the bedroom and stopped. She didn't know the
man, but did Zachary? The woman in the music
store said Zach looked like the man. What if they
were cousins or brothers? There were plenty of
people who didn't connect her to Sabra.

She plopped down in a chair and gnawed on
her lower lip. Just another reason why she
shouldn't have become intimate with Zach until
they knew each other better. But if she was honest

with herself, and she tried to be, she wouldn't have a problem with them becoming lovers if they hadn't had a fight.

Just thinking about Rolling Deep spiked her temper. He'd produced some of the top artists in the industry. He'd even done a country album. Some called him brilliant and gifted, yet he was known for all-night parties, hanging out in nightclubs and with people with unsavory reputations. Although she wasn't entirely pleased with the producer for her last two albums, she wanted nothing to do with Rolling Deep.

The cell phone in her tote rang. She jumped and began frantically digging inside. When the phone proved elusive, she stood and dumped everything onto the chair seat. Picking it up, she quickly flipped it open and answered. "Hello."

"Hi, Laurel."

Laurel's shoulders sagged at the sound of her sister's voice. She leaned against back of the sofa. "Hello, Sabra."

"You certainly sound excited to hear from me. You were having fun. Your vacation turn sour on you?"

Laurel blew out a breath, came to her feet, and walked through the house to the enclosed backyard with an infinity pool. It was peaceful and quiet there with the native plants and giant urns of flowers, yet it did nothing to soothe her jagged nerves. "Yes."

There was a slight pause. "Something tells me there's a man involved. Before today each time

I've called you've been rushing here or there and always happy."

Laurel sat on a lounge chair. Sabra had been on her own since she was twenty and had more experience dealing with men. "We had a fight."

"Back up," Sabra said. "I want details."

Laurel flushed. Sabra might be her sister, but she wasn't getting the intimate details. "We met the night after I arrived. We shared a table since there wasn't one available, and we've been sort of hanging out together."

"I think there's more, but I'll let it slide. So what happened to change things?" her sister asked.

"A silly argument over nothing," Laurel said and went on to explain. She ended by saying, "I was just thinking before you called that they might be related. Perhaps that's why he became so upset with me."

"Laurel, if someone insulted the conductor of the New York Philharmonic—whom you worked with last year and loved every demanding second, every grueling practice—how would you react?"

"The conductor, unlike this R.D. person, has an impeccable reputation," Laurel pointed out.

"You're going by what you've heard or read, and this might sound traitorous, but you are a bit rigid in your choice of music," Sabra said. "You never wanted to take a break and dance with me, Mama, and Dad. It was all I could do to teach you how to dance."

Laurel's eyes closed. "I always thought there was more time."

"Laurel, I didn't mean to make you sad. Dad and I understood. He was so proud of you," Sabra said. "Your profession required hours of practice, mine didn't. And even with all the time I spent with Dad, I still wish we had more. It's natural to feel the way you do."

"I miss him so much."

"I do, too," Sabra confessed softly. "And that's a good thing. Dad was loved and he was happy. He did everything in his power to ensure we were taken care of and happy."

A wistful sigh drifted past Laurel's lips. "He was a great dad."

"And he liked music," Sabra reminded her. "All types."

"I think Zach does as well. Although he doesn't play professionally, he's dynamite on the guitar," Laurel said. "Everyone in the music shop was spellbound."

"What does he do?"

"I don't know. He appears successful. He said his family was privileged. The night we met, he said he didn't want to think about work and decided to play hooky and asked me if I wanted to play with him," Laurel explained. "Since I wanted him to see me as a woman and not the renowned classical violinist, I agreed. It worked until we had the argument."

"So, how are you going to fix things?"

Laurel watched a bee fly from one flower to the other and sighed. "I guess I might be a bit rigid, but I don't know if I can."

"And you won't know until you try. All you have to do is ask yourself if he's worth the effort. If you never saw him again, would you be okay with it?"

Laurel's stomach knotted just thinking about not seeing Zach again. "I like him. A lot. He's drop-dead gorgeous with a hot body, but he's so unconscious about it and so easy to be with."

Sabra laughed. "The first time I saw Pierce I practically drooled, but thank goodness he has other worthwhile qualities."

"So does Zach. He's kind, gentle, and patient. He's so considerate. He doesn't do it because I'm this famous person, he just does it."

"Oh, Laurel. I can hear the excitement in your voice. The right man will do that for you. All I can say is, it's about time. Get off this phone and go show Zach he'll be miserable without you."

"But—"

"No buts," Sabra said, cutting her off. "Live. There's more to life than performing on the stage."

"Is that why you refused to let me bring my violin?"

"Yes. You would have spent time in your room playing. Instead you met Zach, and I can't wait to meet him, too," Sabra told her, laughing.

"I want you to." Laurel came to her feet. "He's wonderful. Thanks as always for being the best big sister ever."

"Go. Bye."

Laurel shut the cell phone off. The smile slowly faded. How was she going to apologize to Zach?

* * *

He'd lost her.

Zach sat on the steps of the cottage and looked out at the calm, endless sea. He finally realized that nothing he could do or say would change Laurel's mind about R.D. The smart thing to do was pack and leave.

Earlier, he'd dragged his suitcase from the closet and tossed a few things inside, but that was as far as he'd gotten. Just the thought of leaving her, of never seeing her again, twisted his insides. He wanted to produce her album, but even more he wanted her to be his, free and open and loving.

He wasn't sure when his plan had changed. No, that was a lie. From the moment she'd looked up at him, he'd been lost. The first kiss had put a lock on it. After they'd made love, the key had been tossed away. She was important to him.

And she couldn't stand him.

It didn't matter that she was wrong. She was so set in her mind that nothing he did or said would sway her. If he tried, she'd condemn him within seconds. Either way, it was the same.

She was lost to him.

The ache in his chest deepened with each breath. He'd always had hope that he could get her to change her mind about R.D., but her adamancy this afternoon had shown he was wrong.

He scrubbed his hand over his face. He hadn't meant to become angry with her, but it was so unfair of her to go on rumors instead of facts.

Desperation had also played a part in his reaction. If he couldn't get her to at least consider she might be wrong, she'd hate him when he told her the truth.

And she'd never want to see him again.

He loved a woman who despised the man she didn't know he was. The realization didn't surprise him. What did surprise him was the way he'd handled things. He was a persuasive, charming guy. He had to be in his line of work. Some of his clients had egos the size of Texas.

But he couldn't charm Laurel or persuade her that she was wrong. He had boxed himself into a corner with no way out. He hadn't the foggiest notion how to straighten things out between them. The truth would anger and embarrass her. She'd probably think he had used sex to try to control her.

Loving her was the most honest thing he'd ever done. She was so easy to love, to cherish. Having her awaken in his arms was sheer bliss. She was so different from other women, so unselfish.

His jaw clenched. His head bowed until his chin almost touched his chest. He'd been the selfish one. Taking her virginity, betraying her trust. Once he told her his true identity, she'd be even more sure that the lies she'd heard about him were true.

And he couldn't blame her.

"Zach."

His head snapped up. Laurel stood a short

distance away. She looked wary. Happiness swept through him. He stood, then remembered the lies and closed his eyes.

"Please don't be angry with me," she said. "My sister reminded me that I can be a bit rigid when it comes to music."

His eyes popped open. "I'm not angry at you."

She took another few steps toward him. "I almost didn't make it. The security guards stopped the cabdriver, but then they let me go when I told them who I was and that I was coming to see you."

She had no idea that her name carried just as much clout as his. Perhaps more. When the lies came out, it was going to be a royal mess. He'd involved too many people. "I'm sorrier than you'll ever know."

A smile broke over her beautiful face. He'd carry it in his heart forever.

"I shouldn't have been so adamant about a person I know nothing about." She dug into her bag and pulled out a handful of Rap and hard rock CDs. "I went by the record shop and purchased these. I thought we could listen to them together."

She was all that he ever wanted even before he knew what that was. And he had to let her go.

She took a tentative step closer. "Let's go back to before we got into an argument about a man neither of us knows."

Here was his chance. He opened his mouth.

"I-I know we haven't known each other long,

but—but I—I feel—" She laughed nervously. "I usually can express myself better, but this is new to me. I've never felt this way before. I told my sister about you, and she said I should apologize. You're always so thoughtful. You still want to be with me, don't you?"

"Always." He closed the distance and pulled her into his arms. She'd just opened herself to him. He couldn't tell her now. It would hurt her too badly, especially after she'd told her sister about him. But he could give her his one unshakable truth. "I've never felt this way about a woman before. I don't want to lose you."

Her body trembled against his. Her arms clutched him. "You won't. I told my sister what a wonderful, caring man you are."

Oh, Lord. How was he going to keep from hurting her? With each innocent word, she made things harder.

"Zach?" she said, her voice uncertain.

Somehow he'd find a way. He had to. His head lifted. "You game to go watch the fireworks at the Mayan ruins?"

"You don't want to listen to the music?"

For once, music was the farthest thing from his mind. "It can wait. Remember, I promised to take you."

A smile blossomed on her face. "And you're a man of your word. A rarity these days."

She was killing him, and he deserved every slice to his heart. "Let's go." Taking her hand, he started for the Jeep.

*   *   *

It was close to one in the morning when Zach walked Laurel to her door. He'd gone over different ways of telling her the truth, but each time he'd thought of confessing his identity, she'd smile at him, happy and content, and the words would stick in his throat.

Opening her bag, she handed him the key. He opened the door and handed it back to her instead of opening it wider and following her in as he'd done in the past.

"You must be tired so I'll take off. The Mayan jungle tour tomorrow starts at eight. I'll pick you up at seven to give us time for breakfast."

She smiled provocatively up at him. "We can always cancel."

"I kind of wanted to see it." Leaning over, he kissed her on the cheek. "Good night. I'll see you in the morning."

She stared up at him with questions in her eyes. "All right. Good night."

The door closed, and he went back to his Jeep. He had to find a way to tell her. Tomorrow. He'd tell her tomorrow.

Something is wrong.

Laurel had tossed and turned most of the night. Waiting for Zach that morning, she felt tense instead of happy. She hadn't missed Zach's staring at her most of the night instead of at the fireworks, his brow furrowed. Something had changed between them. He'd said he didn't want to lose her, but he'd left her on the doorstep.

She jumped as the doorbell rang. Perhaps he was having second thoughts after all and just didn't know how to tell her. The bell rang again. She came to her feet and answered the door.

"Good morning," Zach greeted her.

"Good morning." Laurel felt a knot in her throat. The heart-stopping smile, the barely contained desire she'd seen on his face the past few days, was gone. "I think I'll take a pass on today," she told him.

"What?" He came inside, shutting the door after him. "Do you feel all right?"

"Yes." She hoped the smile on her face didn't look as brittle as she felt. "I think I'll take a break and just rest for the day. You go on."

"I'm not going without you. And I'm certainly not going off someplace when you're not feeling well," he said.

"You don't have to pretend you care," she said, wanting him to leave before the tears clogging her throat worsened. "You couldn't get out of here fast enough last night."

He tensed. "It was late, and you were tired."

"It never mattered before." She went to the door. "I won't keep you."

He stared at her a long time, then started for the door—or so she thought. At the last second, he pulled her into his arms, his mouth finding hers. She gasped in surprise and his tongue swept inside, thrusting and dueling with hers. Protests stumbled and died. She was caught up in the pleasure sweeping through her.

He lifted his head, his breathing harsh. "I want you. I couldn't sleep last night because I wanted to be here. If I had been, you wouldn't have gotten any sleep."

She felt the proof of his desire, frank and un-ashamed, nudging her. She wouldn't back down. "You kept looking at me last night and frowning." She hated the quiver in her voice.

"You're right." His hand tunneled though her hair. "I'm trying to figure out something. I didn't expect you. It threw me."

"Is there someone else?"

His face and hand gentled. "No. There hasn't been anyone in a very long time and I haven't wanted anyone—until I saw you."

Her forehead rested on his chest. "I thought you wanted to end things."

His thumb lifted her head. "I've never felt this way about anyone."

She stared into dark eyes swirling with passion. "Me, neither. I guess that why it's so scary. I don't want to be hurt."

His forehead touched hers. His hands trembled. "I don't want that, either. Please always remember that."

She pushed out of his arms. Fear flashed in his eyes. She had her answer. Whatever it was bothering him, he did care about her. Continuing to the sofa, she picked up her bag and put on her hat. "We better hurry if we're going to eat first."

Relief spread over his face. "You wearing your swimsuit under there?"

She pushed over the V-neck of her boxy chocolate top to show a white shoulder strap. "Yep."

"Did you get your sunscreen?"

"Got it. Let's go. It's going to be a wonderful day." Kissing him on the cheek, she sailed out of the door.

Six

How can I tell her now? Zach thought as he mounted the ATV and Laurel got on behind him. Her tears had made his gut knot. It had been hard leaving her last night, but he felt it was the right thing to do under the circumstances. Trying to come up with a way to let know her who he was, he hadn't even attempted to sleep.

"This is going to be fun," Laurel said, her arms around his waist.

"Hold me close," Zach said. "I hear the terrain can get a bit rough."

Laughing, she tightened her grip. "At least if I fall off, I won't have far to fall."

"Just hold on," he told her, and started out behind the ATVs in front of him. There were eight couples in all, and they were third in line. The tour began within the dense jungles of the Mayan Riviera. Sunlight barely reached them through the tall trees with branches that met and tangled.

He hadn't gone thirty feet before he decided this was another bad idea. With each sway of their bodies, Laurel's breasts rubbed against his back. He was in the V of her legs. It was pure sensual torture. All he could do was grit his teeth and hold tightly to the handles. Perhaps it was fitting punishment for not being up front with her.

The first break didn't come until an hour later. They stopped at a small village. Unlike all of the other couples, neither he nor Laurel played in the cenote, a surface connection to subterranean water, or took a bath in the crystal waters of the underground river—one of many on the Yucatán Peninsula. There were almost no surface rivers and few lakes due to the area's relatively sparse rainfall.

Laurel leaned against him as she drank her bottled water. "There is no way I'm getting in that water after the guide said they'd discovered sacrificial objects in there." She shivered and stepped closer to him. "Mayans made human sacrifices as well. I guess the others are more adventurous than we are."

"Must be," Zach said, and sipped his water. He hadn't gone swimming because he would have had to walk stooped over for fifty yards to get there. His only hope was that the underground river in a cave on the next stop was closer to the road.

"Everyone back on," the guide told them. "It's time to go."

Zach quickly finished his water, then stuck his and Laurel's empty bottles back in the backpack on the ATV. He wanted to whimper when Laurel climbed on behind him. *Please, let the water be closer to the road,* he thought, and pulled out to follow the other couples.

A couple of hours later they stopped at the cave where they could swim in the underground river. Zach wasn't the only male slowly getting off the ATV and heading for the water to cool off. He gritted his teeth and removed his jeans and shirt . . . and then he was in blissfully cool, clear water up to his waist. He didn't turn around until Laurel tapped him on the back.

"Cold showers aren't what they're cracked up to be?"

His laugh was ragged, but he pulled her into his arms for the sheer pleasure of holding her and to keep his eyes off her breasts in the white bikini top. "No, they're not."

She wrapped her arms lightly around his waist. Other couples splashed and played in the water around them. "This is an all-day thing, right?"

"Right," he answered, wondering how he was going to stand being in a state of arousal so long.

She leaned back. "You planning to leave me at the door tonight?"

Breath shuddered through his lungs. "If I do, it won't mean I don't wish I was with you."

"We'll see." She tilted her head to one side. "Would it be better if I drove?"

He didn't even have to think about it. "Worse probably."

"Sorry," she said. "I guess renting a jet ski before we leave is out of the question."

His eyes narrowed. "Those things are too dangerous. People turn into speed demons."

"Don't tell me you've never ridden on one?" she asked.

"I have, and we're still not getting on one," he said adamantly. "Accidents can happen. Unfortunately too many people have been injured or run over on jet skis."

"I don't suppose we're going to try the aerial zip-line, either?" she asked.

Zach had glanced at the cables suspended over another cenote as he headed for the underground river. "You could lose your grip and fall. But if you want to try, we will."

She gazed at him. "I'd rather stay here and let you hold me."

"My thoughts exactly." He'd remain as hard as a rock, but it was worth it.

A little after sunset, Zach hurried Laurel to the Jeep as fast as he could considering his uncomfortable erection. He jammed the key in the ignition and spun out of the gravel parking lot.

His hands clamped on the steering wheel, he stared straight ahead. Once they were ready to come back, Laurel had removed her loose-fitting top. The bikini top pushing up her high, firm breasts almost had his tongue hanging out.

He didn't know if Laurel brushed her body against his on purpose after they spoke in the waterfall, but every time they took a break and removed their helmets, she kissed and blew on his ear. Her hands also had a tendency to drift lower than his waist. They never reached his groin, just his thigh—which made him harder because he wanted her hand on him.

He'd looked over his shoulder at her the second time it had happened. She'd stared back, bold and daring. She didn't plan for him to leave her at the door tonight. She was in control again, sure of herself and enjoying every second.

In a screech of brakes, Zach stopped in front of her condo. He met her on the sidewalk. He fumbled to unlock her front door. Finally it swung open and they were inside. The last coherent thought before he desperately reached for her was that it wasn't power that drove her, but her need to know how desperately he wanted her.

They barely made it to the bed, hastily discarding clothes, kissing as they went. She had no more than hit the bed before he'd put on a condom and surged into her. The pleasure of her tightly holding him within her body almost made him give in to the need for release. Almost.

"Hold on," he murmured as he locked his mouth on hers and loved her.

The pace was fast. She met each thrust, her legs locked around his waist. The orgasm burst through him. Their mingled cries of pleasure echoed through the room.

* * *

Everything was back to the way it had been. Her breathing finally slowing to normal, Laurel snuggled closer to Zach, felt his strong arms close possessively around her. He brushed his lips against her shoulder, her hair.

"You're incredible and beautiful. You're the most amazing thing that has ever happened to me."

"You're pretty incredible yourself." Laurel hugged his arms, hugged the words to her. She couldn't imagine being that aggressive before, but a couple of times she'd caught the sadness in Zach's eyes and knew he was thinking about them. She'd wanted him to know that, for her, this wasn't a vacation fling. For him, she was willing to take a chance. She was falling in love, was probably already there.

"I'm leaving in a few days," she said softly.

His arms tightened. "I want to see you after we leave here."

The breath she hadn't known she was holding fluttered out over her lips. "I'd like that. I'll be in Los Angeles for the next couple of months."

"A lot of musicians and movie stars live there," he said. "I'm surprised you feel so strongly about rap music."

She rolled on top of him and shook her head. "We're not discussing music. I don't want to get into another argument."

The corner of his mouth tilted upward. "I noticed you haven't mentioned playing the CDs you brought to the cottage."

Laurel wrinkled her nose and smiled. "Would you believe I forgot?"

"No."

She kissed him playfully on the lips. "Then let's agree to stay away from subjects that we're not going to agree on. I want our last days together here to be happy ones."

Frown lines pleated his brow. "I—"

"Please," she said. "I have some things to tell you and I'd rather wait until the last night. That way, if things fall apart, I'll be on my way home." She tried to say the words teasingly, but her voice trembled.

His hand tenderly cupped her cheek. "All right. I'll cook dinner at the cottage and we'll talk. Now go to sleep."

Smiling, she lay her head down, listening to the steady beat of his heart. Things would work out. He wouldn't freak, like a couple of men she'd met, when he learned who she was. He certainly wouldn't want to use her simply because he didn't know her identity. Smiling, she drifted off to sleep.

The next day they went horseback riding and later played in the ocean like two kids. They made love in a deserted cove, then gathered driftwood and started a fire. Blissfully peaceful and happy, they watched the sun set before going back to the cottage. Showering together, they made love again.

He made them an omelet, which they ate in bed, laughing and talking about the day. That night she went to sleep in his arms.

The following morning, they went snorkeling, holding hands when possible, and delighting in the colorful array of sea life. When night came, they dined at the Seascape before returning to her place. It seemed natural for them to undress each other and go to bed. Their lovemaking held a hint of desperation, as if both of them knew their talk the next night might tear them apart.

The next day he left her condo and went home to change. She joined him an hour later at the cottage. Both wanted to spend the last day by themselves. He took her home around six with her promise to be back by eight for their dinner date at the cottage. After tonight, there would be no more secrets between them.

Returning from taking Laurel home, Zach couldn't remember ever being this nervous as he went about preparing dinner. Tonight would determine their future together. Had he taken the easy way out by waiting as she'd wanted? He hoped not.

Shaking his head, he went to check on the fish he was grilling. While in the kitchen, he picked up the bouquet of cut flowers in a crystal vase and placed them on the table. Reaching over, he adjusted the tapered white candles in the crystal holders again. He wanted everything as romantic and perfect as possible. His often-repeated prayer as he went about getting things ready was that she'd listen and believe him.

He picked up the white linen napkin by her place setting to check again that the turquoise bracelet and earrings were still beneath. He hadn't had them gift-wrapped. He hoped she'd be pleased, and maybe a bit shaky, which would give him just enough time to slip the bracelet on her wrist, kiss each ear, and have her put the earrings on.

He turned at the knock on the door. Despite the apprehension he felt, he smiled and went back inside. Laurel was so proper. She always knocked. He'd told her to just come on in, but he knew she wouldn't. She was too much of a southern lady.

Still smiling, he reached for the doorknob. "Hon—What are you doing here?"

Lee "Big Man" Wilson, a pop singer whose last album had bombed because he'd refused to listen to Zach, grinned. Caps flashed in a dark chocolate face. "Hey, dog. You're a hard man to find."

"That's the way I wanted it," Zach said, not moving from the door.

Big Man's smile faltered. "Come on, man. I need you. My record label said you can write your own ticket."

"There's not enough money in LA for me to work with you again, Lee. I thought I made that clear. You questioned every suggestion during the recording session, and you did the same thing all through the mix and mastering. You made the entire process grueling."

Lee waved his hand dismissively, gold and diamonds glinting on four fingers. Even in the tropical heat, he wore an Armani suit, silk shirt, and tie. He'd come from a middle-class family, but his bio said he'd been reared in the hood by drug-selling parents.

He liked the finer things and spent lavishly. His sales were in the toilet and his record label wasn't happy. "I might have held the reins a bit tight, but you sign back on and you'll be the man."

"No."

A shadow moved. Zach's head jerked up, thinking it was Laurel. Instead it was two of Lee's bodyguards. "How did you find me and get through security?" Zach asked.

Lee grinned again. "I know people."

Zach didn't buy it. "No one would have told you where I was. So you must have hired someone to find me by tracing my credit card activity." That wiped the grin off Lee's smug face. "Bad decision. You might have been able to get past security with lies, but you won't like the consequences."

The bodyguards moved to stand beside Lee. "Rolling Deep, watch what you say to Big Man and step back," one of the men warned.

"You'd do better to take that advice yourself," Zach said. "Whatever lie you told to get past security is being checked and when it can't be confirmed, you're going to be over your head in trouble."

Lee waved another dismissive hand. "Rolling Deep, you or no one else can scare me. I come and go as I please."

"What—what did he call you?"

Zach's head snapped around. Laurel was standing there, a few feet in front of Kyle. She looked stricken. Yesterday, when she'd come by herself, Kyle had walked her to the cottage. Zach cursed under his breath and quickly went down the steps to her. She held up her hand and stepped back when he reached for her.

"Please, just listen. I was going to tell you tonight," he told her, clenching his fists. "If I had told you who I was, you wouldn't have given me the time of day."

"You lied to me!" she cried, her voice and body shaking. "To think I bragged to my sister what a wonderful, honest man you were."

"Having women trouble, R.D.?" Lee sneered. "Produce my album and I'll get you all the honeys you need. Forget about her. You don't need her."

Zach whirled, moved past the bodyguards, and slammed his fist into Lee's face. A hand clamped on his shoulder, but then it was gone. Zach kept his angry gaze on Lee, who was sprawled on the ground. "Shut your mouth and leave."

"You heard the man." Kyle stepped around Zach and jerked Lee none too gently to his feet.

"The boss takes a dim view of people harassing guests, and a dimmer view of liars. His sister didn't send you."

Lee tried to pull away and found it impossible. "Do you know who I am?"

Kyle rolled off stats on the man, then leaned in closer. "You just pissed off the wrong man. You'd better get back to LA and enjoy it while you can." He released Lee, who took off. His two body-guards were already gone.

Zach glanced around. There was no sign of Laurel.

"Looks like that loudmouth isn't the only one in for a butt-load of trouble," Kyle told Zach, but he didn't hear it because he was already running toward his Jeep.

Laurel was shaking so badly, she couldn't get the key into the lock. How could she have been such a fool? She'd believed every lie he'd fed her.

"I'll get it." The man who had driven her back to the condo gently removed the key from her hand, unlocked the door, and handed the key back to her.

She clenched the cold metal in her palm and willed herself not to cry. Her eyes stung. The lump in her throat grew.

"The jet taking you back is already en route and should land in an hour. I was told to let you know that you can take off then or leave as scheduled at ten in the morning," the man continued.

Her head came up. Something didn't make

sense. He worked for the owner of the estate Zach was staying on. He'd been the one to stop her the first time she visited Zach at the cottage, then waved her on once she identified herself and told him where she was heading.

She'd thought since she'd seen Kyle the last time she'd visited Zach in the evening, and he'd walked her to cottage tonight, that the far-reaching wealth of Blade Navarone, coupled with the dangerous intensity of Rio, had not only allowed her access but also allowed both security teams to work together. Now she wasn't sure.

"How do you know about the jet? Aren't you a guard for the owner of the estate we just left?"

His expression unchanged, he said, "Blade Navarone owns the estate and the jet that is taking you back."

Surprise widened Laurel's eyes and bunched her brow. She massaged her temples. Nothing made sense . . . except she'd been a fool. The only reason Zach had been with her was to get her to let him produce her next album or to humiliate her since she'd refused to even speak to him. But how did he know Blade?

Like a starry-eyed fool, she'd walked straight into Zach's plan. She just hoped Blade's security team was discreet. She had no such hopes about the man who'd revealed Zach's identity or his two bodyguards. She'd be splattered across the media and TMZ. Everyone would be laughing at her. She had to leave LA as soon as possible and return to Nashville. "I'd like to return when the jet lands."

"Kyle will pick you up and take you to the airport," he told her. "Is there anything else?"

She heard the screech of tires and saw Zach jump out of the Jeep and run toward her. She started to rush inside, but she stiffened her body instead. She wouldn't let him see how badly he'd hurt her. Besides, there were questions she wanted answers to.

"Laurel, please let me explain." Zach reached for her.

She stepped back. She never wanted his hands on her again. "How did you get on the Navarone estate?"

"Let's go inside, and I'll answer all the questions you have," he pleaded, reaching for her again.

Again she evaded him. "Just tell me."

He shoved his hand through his hair. "My sister, Paige, is married to Shane Elliott. He was head of security before he resigned and Rio took over."

"So you knew who I was from the beginning," she guessed. "You planned everything."

"Yes, but—"

Laurel turned and opened the door and let the tears fall.

In desperation, Zach reached for Laurel and found the silent man who had been standing with her when he arrived blocking his path.

"Get out of my way," Zach said through clenched teeth.

"If she doesn't want to see you, that's how it has to be," the broad-shouldered man said, his voice quiet and calm, his gaze unwavering. He was six foot three of solid muscle dressed in black.

Zach's fists flexed. "I know you can take me out, but I'm going to talk to her one way or the other."

"Not tonight, unless she gives the okay."

"Get out of my way," Zach repeated. He couldn't get over the shattered look on Laurel's face. He could well imagine what she was thinking, and it tore at his heart. He reached for the man.

"Don't you think you've caused enough problems?" Kyle said from behind him in a lazy drawl.

Zach spun and faced the new adversary. "Tell him to move."

"Hugh is following orders, and Shane is not pleased at the moment with his brother-in-law and might not mind if you tangled with Hugh. On the other hand, I understand his wife is very fond of her big brother and would mind. If she's unhappy, then Shane is going to be. He's not a man I want to rile. Do yourself and all of us a favor and go home. She's not in the mood to listen."

"I have to explain." Zach drew in a shuddering breath. "Please."

"Personally, I don't like my butt in a sling, and that's exactly where you put it. We backed off as

Rio ordered, and it blew up in all of our faces. Shane will meet you head-on, but Rio—" Kyle shook his head. "You better pray he believes you and it's enough."

"I don't give a damn whether he does or not," Zach said. "All I care about is Laurel."

Kyle studied him. "Be here at nine in the morning. The jet leaves at ten to take her back to LA. If you can get her to listen, fine. If not, I wouldn't want to be you."

"All I care about is Laurel," Zach said again, looking at the closed door over Hugh's shoulder. "Whatever happens, I couldn't feel any worse. I hurt her. I never got a chance to tell her I love her." Pulling the keys to the Jeep from his pocket, he handed them back to Kyle and walked away.

Laurel couldn't see what she was throwing in the direction of the suitcase on the bed. She'd been so sure about him and so horribly wrong. Her tears blinded her. She'd actually thought she was in love.

Clutching a pair of slacks, she closed her eyes. How could she have been so brainless.

Her cell phone rang and she ignored it. She didn't have anything to say to a despicable man like Rolling Deep. He was just as unconscionable and unsavory as she'd thought.

The phone on the nightstand rang. She stared in that direction, trying to remember if she'd ever given Zach the phone number to the condo. Suddenly the doorbell rang.

Her hands clenched. There was no reason for anyone besides Zach to be at her door. She should have asked the guard to stay.

The doorbell came again with the ringing of her cell and the phone on the desk. Zach could be behind two of them, but not all three. She fished her cell out of her purse and saw UNKNOWN on her caller ID. She, Sabra, and their mother had unlisted phone numbers. A knock accompanied the ringing of the doorbell.

Cautiously, she moved to the front room. "Yes?"

"Ms. Raineau, your sister is trying to reach you by phone."

The phone in her hand rang again. She connected.

"Honey, I'm sorry," Sabra said quickly, her voice teary. "Everyone is upset about what he pulled."

"Everyone," Laurel repeated and closed her eyes. Of course Kyle had notified Rio, who'd called Shane and Blade. Blade had told Sierra and she had called her brother Pierce, who'd told Sabra, who had called their mother. They all knew how gullible she'd been.

"Pierce and I are flying out to LA tonight. We'll meet you there. They'll just have to shoot around me tomorrow. Pierce got Mother a reservation for a late flight out of Louisville."

"No, please, Sabra. I know you and Mama mean well, but I—I'd really like to be alone right now." Somehow Laurel managed to get the words past the growing lump in her throat. She didn't want to see pity in the faces of her mother or sister. She just wanted to go somewhere, pull the covers over her head, and not have to think or talk. "Please tell Mother not to come back."

"You shouldn't be alone," Sabra insisted. "I could kill him!"

"We'll see that he gets what's coming to him," Pierce said, his voice tight and filled with promise. He sounded so clear he must have been standing beside Sabra. Most likely with his arm around her. That was what Laurel wanted—complete love and devotion. She'd ended up with betrayal.

"No, please. Just let it go," Laurel whispered, her arm across her churning stomach. "I trusted the wrong man. My mistake. I don't want anyone else involved."

"It might be too late," Sabra said.

"What—what do you mean?" Laurel gripped the phone, not liking the sound of that.

"You're family," Pierce told her. "No one, absolutely no one messes with our women. Zachary crossed a line, and it's going to be pointed out to him."

Laurel tried again. "Let it go, please."

"Too late. The wheels are already in motion," Pierce said.

Zachary hired a taxi to take him back to the cottage to pack. He didn't see any of the guards, but he had no doubts that they were watching. Asking the cab to wait, he walked the short distance from the main house. He wouldn't have been surprised to find his clothes already packed and on the porch. They weren't.

He almost wished they were. He didn't want to go inside. Too many memories waited to assail and taunt him. He'd blown it big-time. His fear of losing Laurel had come to fruition. What scared the crap out of him was that he might not be able to get her to listen and forgive him. Once she left Mexico she'd be lost to him.

He had another big problem: his sister Paige. She'd trusted him, helped him, and looked up to him. How could he have screwed things up so badly? At least he had the answer to that question. He hadn't wanted to hurt Laurel, had kept thinking he'd eventually find the right words. Instead it had all came crashing down on him.

A foot inside he smelled the fish. He went to the kitchen and found the fire turned off. Kyle probably. Disposing of the fish and the rest of the food he'd prepared, Zach went to the terrace to clear the table. His gaze was drawn to the napkin and the jewelry beneath.

One day, he promised himself, he'd slip the bracelet on her wrist, the earrings on her ears. If he didn't believe that, he wasn't sure he could go on. Putting the pieces into his pocket, he quickly finished, packed his suitcase and left.

His plane didn't leave until late the next day. He'd sent his travel agent a text message to get him out on an earlier flight, no matter the carrier.

In the meantime he was going to head back to Laurel's place and wait on the off chance Kyle hadn't been truthful with him.

Arriving back at the condo in the taxi, Zach saw a dim light on in the front room and no guards. This was his chance, and he was taking it. "Wait here," he told the driver.

Opening the door, he quickly went down the walk and rang the doorbell, rang again when there was no answer.

He checked his watch. He'd been gone for less than an hour. He looked around, then tested the door. It opened. Even as it did, he berated himself and the security detail. He had made her forget to lock the door, but they were supposed to protect her.

He'd taken two steps when the overhead light came on. He swung his head around to see Rio standing by the light switch, his gaze piercing. "Where is she?"

"Gone."

Zach spun around and reached for the door.

"You won't find her."

Zach slammed the door and walked across the room to face Rio. "Then tell me where she is."

Nothing moved on Rio. It was like looking into a mirror reflection. Zach got the impression of danger and a keen intelligence. "You betrayed a trust."

"I made a mistake. Nothing you can say or do can make me feel worse," he said.

"I wouldn't be so sure about that."

Zach blinked. A chill raced through him.

"You hurt a woman entrusted to me to watch over," Rio said slowly, his voice devoid of warmth and inflection. "Be glad I've seen the look on your face before or we'd test your theory."

Zach hadn't the foggiest notion what Rio was talking about, but there was something more important that needed to be said. "Lee Wilson and his goons were there. Kyle threatened him, but I don't know if it worked. Lee is the vengeful type. He's pissed because I refused to produce his next album. He'll shoot off his mouth and try to get back at me by hurting Laurel. You can't let that happen."

"Already taken care of." Stepping around Zack, Rio walked to the door. "You have two weeks to make things right or you'll see me again." Opening the door, he was gone.

Zach again gave points to his little sister for standing up to Rio, no easy feat. He'd never seen eyes that hard and flat. Zach believed every word Rio said. He'd be in his face in two weeks, but before then he'd be in Lee's and his two goons'. For that, Zach would let Rio do his worst to him.

Now he had to call Paige. He pulled out his BlackBerry and dialed her home phone number. He wasn't looking forward to the conversation.

"Zach, how could you?"

There was censure and condemnation in her voice. He'd never heard either directed at him before from Paige. "I didn't mean for this to happen."

"You betrayed my trust. How do you think I felt when Shane told me what had happened?" Paige said. "I helped you hurt Laurel. You used Shane as well."

He didn't think it possible to feel worse, but he did. "Paige, please, listen. I might have come to Mexico with the intention of getting Laurel to let me produce her album, but that changed when I met her. I care about her. I didn't tell her who I was because I was afraid of losing her."

"Two weeks. Fix it or else," Shane said.

"Rio already delivered the message," Zach snapped. What the hell did they think he was trying to do?

"Good thing he did, or I'd be knocking on your door and, when you answered, it wouldn't be pretty," Shane continued. "Count yourself lucky that you're Paige's brother and she loves you."

Zach had had enough. "I didn't want this to happen," he almost shouted. "I'm trying to fix this, but Kyle gave me wrong information and Laurel is gone."

"Don't try. Do. Two weeks." The line went dead.

Zach hung up the phone and headed out the door. He wasn't worried about Rio's or Shane's threats. His fear was that Laurel was lost to him. By the time he reached LA, he had to have a plan that would keep her there until he made her understand.

Arriving at the airport, one idea kept running through his mind. It had the best chance for success, but it was tricky. The plan could very well widen the chasm between them even farther. Could he risk it?

Getting out of the taxi, he wasn't sure he had a choice.

Seven

Laurel rose from her seat on the jet as soon as Rio came through the hatch. He didn't look any different from when he'd left thirty long minutes ago to "take care of something." "Is Zach all right?"

"Depends." Rio closed and locked the door himself, then spoke to the waiting flight attendant. "We're ready for takeoff."

"Yes, sir." She went to the cockpit.

"Buckle up." Rio moved to a seat on the other side of the jet at an angle from her.

"I—" Laurel began; then she heard the engines start. She took her seat and buckled her seat belt. Rio wouldn't talk until he was ready. Kyle and Hugh weren't afraid of him, but they obviously respected him and didn't know what to expect when Rio came off the jet to meet them.

Without a word, Kyle had met him at the bottom of the steps. The conversation was short, their voices so low she couldn't hear what was being said. She'd tried. She hated Zach for his lies and deceit, but he hadn't forced her into going to bed with him. She was an adult and had to take responsibility for her actions.

She felt the jet picking up speed and then lifting into the air. She watched Rio the entire time. He stared straight ahead. He remained expressionless. She'd never met anyone so self-contained. Surely something moved him, but nothing showed, not happiness or anger or fear.

His head turned, his gaze locked on her. She leaned back against the seat. She didn't know why. Yes, she did. There was something dangerously menacing about him, but he was a strikingly beautiful man. The combination made you pause.

"Don't worry about Wilson or the men with him talking," he said, his deep voice oddly compelling.

"Wilson?" she asked.

"Lee 'Big Man' Wilson. He's a rapper, and he's the man Zachary Albright punched out tonight for insulting you," Rio answered

Laurel's eyes widened. "Zach hit him?"

"If you had stayed, you would have seen it."

She frowned. She couldn't tell if there was censure in his voice or not. Probably so. Rio didn't appear to have the emotional baggage of others, but then he wouldn't have the joys, either. "How do you plan to keep him from talking?"

"I have ways" came Rio's simple answer.

She believed him. "Is Zach—Zachary all right?" she asked again.

"Depends," Rio answered as before, and then

lifted the top of the laptop on the built-in desk in front of him and began typing. For a man with such large hands, his fingers flew effortlessly and gracefully over the keyboard. He moved the same way, reminding her of a large healthy animal.

"Is he all right?" Laurel repeated, her voice rising in irritation.

Rio looked up. "Are you?"

Laurel felt the hurt, the betrayal, the embarrassment again. "Nothing happened to him."

"You're wrong."

"How can you say that?" she hissed, not caring that her voice carried. "What did he lose?"

"You," Rio said slowly. "He lost you."

Laurel looked away. She hadn't meant anything to Zach. He'd used her. Memories tried to surface—the tender way he'd held her, the way he'd tried to please her, looked after her—but she ruthlessly squashed them. He'd played her, as they said. She was through with him.

She thought Rio was perceptive, but obviously she'd been wrong. How could he be if he thought Zach was even a hundredth as miserable and wounded as she was. He was just sorry he'd been found out. She swallowed hard around the lump in her throat.

Somehow she'd forget and move on. She never wanted to see him or hear from him again.

Laurel entered her bedroom in Los Angeles, turned on the lights, then promptly turned them off as she crossed the hardwood floor to the wide bed raised on a dais. Stripping down to her bra and panties, she crawled beneath the covers, drawing the down comforter up to her nose.

She hadn't slept on the plane, and she wasn't sleepy now. She could only hope and pray that neither her mother nor Sabra showed up tomorrow. They'd want to talk, try to console her. Nothing could take away the pain and humiliation she felt.

The cell phone in her purse rang. It had rung every fifteen minutes since they landed. Instead of answering, she'd disconnected the call and phoned her mother, then Sabra, to let them know she had landed and again ask for time. Reluctantly, they'd agreed. While talking, she'd learned that neither of them had called. It was Zach then, and it was him calling now. The ringing stopped.

Throwing back the covers, Laurel flicked on the light and then went to her handbag to retrieve the cell phone and shut it off. Putting it back in her bag, she glanced at the clock: 2:43 AM. She wasn't going to sleep.

Going to her closet, she slipped on a silk robe then moved to the violin case, the only thing on the narrow desk, and opened it. Her unsteady fingers traced the strings, the wood. Picking the instrument up, she tucked the base beneath her chin and began to play a sorrowful piece that tugged at her heart. Tears rolled down her cheeks as she walked to the terrace and kept playing.

* * *

Zach arrived at LAX a little after 2:00 AM. He was on his BlackBerry the moment the flight attendant gave the clearance. He needed every moment to put his plan into motion.

"I care about you, Laurel. Please call me." Zach disconnected the BlackBerry and sat back against the backseat in the Bentley. Toby had picked him up.

He knew she wasn't sleeping any more than he had. He hadn't even tried on the plane. He'd managed to snag the last seat on the last flight leaving for LA that night.

While waiting for his flight, he'd received a phone call from Sabra and Laurel's mother. Knowing he deserved every harsh word they said to him, he'd listened. The difficult part came when her mother had talked of her "baby" and not being able to go to her.

"I hear there's a possibility that you might care about Laurel, that you never intended to hurt her," she said.

"I do. I handled things wrong, but I'm going to do everything in my power to win her back," he said earnestly.

"If you can't, then you and I are going to have a talk." The phone had gone dead.

Laurel was loved, but he knew that it wouldn't help her get past what she saw as his betrayal. When he'd asked Carmen to marry him before he took off to LA, she'd refused in the harshest, most ego-denting way. Nothing Paige or his mother said eased the feelings of dejection, or made him believe his world would ever be the same. His father had said it served him right.

He'd picked up the ring and left the next day for LA as planned. He'd kept the ring with the idea of making it big and then asking Carmen to marry him again. By the time he'd become a success, she was married. He'd donated the ring to a charity auction to help retired musicians, and moved on with his life.

This time he wasn't going anywhere. His feelings weren't going to fade or change. They would only grow stronger. He'd show Laurel that she was the most important thing in the world to him. He had to. He couldn't go on otherwise.

He had one chance to keep Laurel in LA. She'd see it as further evidence that he had an ulterior motive for seeking her out. He might have gone to this extreme length before he saw her sitting at the dining table, kissed her, but after that she, not the album, became the driving reason he wanted to be with her.

Looking down at the BlackBerry a little after eight in his home office, Zach placed another call. It would either bring Laurel back or push her away forever. "David Peterson, Zachary Wilder calling."

Forty-two minutes later Zach was in the backseat of his Bentley. Traffic on the freeway was horrible as usual, but soon they were downtown. Toby found a rare parking space and zipped in. Zach reached for the door the moment he came to a stop. Time wasn't on his side. Laurel would want to go home to Nashville to try to forget him. He couldn't allow that.

He entered the spacious lobby of Arial Records and headed straight for the receptionist. "Zachary Wilder to see Mr. Peterson."

The redhead with spiked hair pressed her hand to enhanced breasts that strained against the red silk blouse she wore. "Certainly, R.D., I mean Mr. Wilder. James will escort you to the fifteenth floor. Ms. Sims, Mr. Peterson's personal assistant, will be waiting for you once you get off the elevator."

"This way, Mr. Wilder," James said. The security guard extended his arm toward the elevator.

"Thank you." Zach saw that another guard was holding the elevator for him. People were grumbling about the elevator not being used, but as he passed the whispers grew louder. He was recognized, and people were speculating on the reason for his visit.

Zach stepped into the chrome-and-glass enclosure. He could just imagine their surprise. He didn't go to CEOs, they came to him. He'd learned early in life that the more inaccessible you were, the greater your value. It was that way in his parents' circle of friends, and even more so in entertainment. People tended to value what they couldn't have.

The doors of the elevator glided open. An attractive brunette in a three-piece business suit extended her hand. "Ms. Sims."

"Yes. Good morning, Mr. Wilder. Mr. Peterson is waiting for you in his office. Please follow me."

"Good morning, and thank you." Zach followed the straight-backed woman down a long hallway lined with photos of recording artists whose albums and songs had gone gold or platinum. It was a respectable showing, but meager when compared with other labels. He noted with pride that Laurel had the most platinum albums.

Arial Records was an old, conservative label that had just started signing pop artists. The potential for growth was there, but their artists needed guidance and exposure. Zach, R.D., could give that to them. Peterson, the newly appointed CEO, had contacted Zach's agent about him producing albums for Arial, but he hadn't been interested.

Until now.

Opening a door, she stepped aside for Zach to enter. He saw three men waiting for him and extended his hand to Peterson, a slim man in his late sixties in a charcoal Brioni suit. The other two were just as well dressed, but stockier in build.

Zach had done a thorough search on the label before he'd had his agent contact Laurel's agent. He knew the man on the left in his early forties was the director of marketing. The other man was the CFO. All three had been with the label less than two years and were reportedly responsible for the new vision and inclusion of once "too progressive" artists.

"Zach Wilder. Thank you, Mr. Peterson, so much for meeting with me on such short notice." Zach extended his hand.

"A pleasure, Mr. Wilder." Peterson's handshake was strong, his gaze direct and friendly. "Since you wanted to talk business I thought it might be a good idea to have Sam Morris, the marketing director, and Ted Keats, the chief financial officer, join us."

"Good thinking," Zack said and shook hands with the other two men. "A pleasure, Mr. Morris. Mr. Keats."

"The pleasure is ours," Morris said, his gaze a little glazed. Zach thought it was probably due to him trying to add up how much Zach's association with the record label would mean in sales. Keats was a little more reserved.

"Let's go into my office," Peterson said. Ms. Sims rushed to open the door. "Do you want coffee or anything?"

"No, thank you, but please go ahead if you want." Zach entered the plush office and took the seat indicated at a polished round oak table with seating for six. Peterson and Morris sat on either side of him.

"Now," Peterson said, as he took a seat and placed his arms on the table. "Your phone call mentioned you had a plan that would be financially beneficial to both of us. I'd like to hear it."

This was it. "I'd like to produce Laurel Raineau's next album."

* * *

Way before the first light of dawn, Laurel decided to be on the first available flight to Nashville before the day was over. A phone call from her agent shortly after noon changed those plans. No matter what Laurel said, her agent insisted the meeting at her house was crucial to her career. The CEO, David Peterson, was coming with her for the meeting at 2:00 PM. Her agent was all aflutter. Peterson didn't go see his clients, they came to him—if he had the time.

Reluctantly, Laurel had agreed and booked the last flight out for Nashville. She'd called her mother and spoken to her briefly. Sabra had been on the set of her new movie, so Laurel had spoken to Pierce.

"Wherever you are, we're coming Wednesday," Pierce said.

Two days. Laurel knew it wasn't a request. She just hoped by then that she'd feel more like seeing someone. She'd hung up the phone and gone to ask the cook to prepare a light snack. People in Los Angeles always seemed to be drinking and eating. She thought of Zach cooking for her, them laughing over the meal, and pushed thoughts of him away. It would take time, but she'd forget him.

When the doorbell rang at exactly two, she was there to answer. Seeing the jovial face of Peterson and the perpetually happy one of her agent, Alice Betts, Laurel let out a relieved sigh. No matter that Rio had assured her that Lee and his men would be silenced, she couldn't keep from worrying. "Good afternoon, Mr. Peterson, Alice. Please come in."

"Hello, Laurel." Alice kissed the air on each side of her cheeks.

Peterson gave her a brief and friendly hug. "Hello, Laurel. You look wonderful as usual. Alice said you just returned from a short vacation."

"Thank you." Laurel smiled. Sabra wasn't the only Raineau with acting ability. "Why don't we go into the solarium? The cook has prepared a light meal, if you're hungry."

Peterson chuckled. "I did miss lunch."

"Same here," Alice said. "Laurel is always the perfect hostess. Comes from her being a southern lady."

"We're proud of her and her music," Peterson said.

"Let's go to the solarium." Laurel led them to one of her favorite rooms in the house. Both she and her mother loved flowers. The high-ceilinged room was filled with them. Today there was also a tray of bite-sized sandwiches and fruit on a side table. "Please help yourself. I've already eaten." Laurel didn't wince at the lie, just waited patiently as Peterson and Alice filled their plates. "What would you like to drink?"

"White wine," Alice said.

"Make that two," Peterson added.

Laurel refused to think of her and Zach sharing a glass of wine in the hammock and watching the sunset. She placed the glasses on the small dining table in the room and waited for them to take their seats before taking her own.

"Laurel, your last album did very well for us." Peterson finished off his sandwich and placed up a bit of salmon on a cracker.

"Platinum." Alice winked at Laurel. "The next one will go double platinum."

"I was happy with gold." Laurel ignored Alice's frown.

"I have every belief that Alice is right." Peterson shoved his plate aside and wiped his hands with the linen napkin.

"I've been thinking that perhaps we should delay going into the studio for a month or so," Laurel said, trying to appear calm instead of desperate.

Her agent looked surprised and stopped eating. Questions swirled in her eyes.

Peterson shook his graying head. "Impossible. As you're aware, the release date of your album is already set. You're scheduled to go into the studio tomorrow."

She was ready for this. "Hall produced my last two albums. He won't mind the delay."

"Hall won't be producing this time," Peterson told her, his blue eyes direct. "We have a rare opportunity, and we need to jump on it."

Laurel's pulse skittered. She willed herself to calm down and not jump to conclusions.

"What is it?" Alice asked, turning to him. "You said you wanted to tell us at the same time."

Peterson linked his hands on the table. "You might be the luckiest musician in this town. Everyone wants him and he wants you."

Laurel's heart lurched. Just hearing the words of a man wanting her shouldn't remind her of Zach and send heat spiraling through her. "Yes. Who?"

"Zach Wilder. Rolling Deep. He came to my office this morning and specifically asked to produce your next album." Peterson grinned and leaned back in the chair. "We've been after him for months for three of our other clients and we've always met with a polite but firm no."

"No." Laurel rose unsteadily to her feet. "I won't work with him."

He frowned. "What?"

"Wilder already tried to get Laurel to work with him." Alice motioned Laurel to take her seat before turning to Peterson. "She refused because of his unsavory reputation."

Peterson waved her words aside and leaned forward once again. "Media hype. Artists are lined up to work with him, but as a free agent he can pick and choose. The word is already out that he was in my office. Since he left, two recording artists we were trying to sign said they'd come on if he produced their album. He's money in the bank."

"No," Laurel repeated, reluctantly sitting down at the repeated motion to do so from her agent. She couldn't let her temper get the best of her.

The smile slid from Peterson's face. "You'll go into the studio tomorrow with Wilder."

"Impossible." Just the thought of seeing Zach made her stomach knot. "There's no way I'm letting him produce my next album."

"Your contract says the studio has final approval on the producer, and it's Wilder." His eyes hard, he turned to the agent. "Tell her."

Alice gulped and looked as if the food she'd eaten might not stay down. "He's right."

Laurel felt her body tremble. She couldn't face him knowing he'd used her. *There has to be a way. Think.* "I don't have to go into the recording studio at the same time. I can just send the files to him. Just like I did with Hall. Wilder can add the instrumentals later."

Peterson was shaking his head before she finished. "Wilder wants to work directly with you. His reason, and it's a good one, is that if he has suggestions on a particular piece, it makes more sense to work on it then."

Her temper flared. "I don't need him telling me how to play the violin!"

"Laurel, I'm sure that isn't what David is implying," Alice soothed.

"No, and since you've had artistic freedom on all of the albums you've done with us, before and after I became CEO, you should know that."

Laurel accepted the reprimand. "Then let me send him the files."

"You'll be in the studio at ten on Tuesday."

He wasn't backing down, and neither was she.

She came to her feet and placed both hands on the tabletop. "This is the last album of my contract. If you force me to go into the studio with him, it will be my last."

Her agent's sharp intake of breath cut through the room.

Peterson shook his head. "You're one of our best-selling artists and we both know it. You've been with us since you went professional. I'd hate to lose you, but if you work with Wilder, he's promised to work with three other artists."

"Is what he wants more important and the lure of his sordid reputation more important than what I want?" Laurel asked. "Alice knows other labels have tried to lure me away, but I've stayed. You can't be man enough to show the same loyalty?"

Alice frantically shook her head. Laurel ignored her.

Anger turning his face red, Peterson slowly came to his feet. "You're upset, Wilder said you would be. He mentioned he had tried to speak with you, but his agent hadn't been able to get past Alice."

Zach hadn't mentioned their affair in Mexico. She was too angry to be thankful.

"He believes in your music. He brought your last recording to show instances where it could be improved on. The mixing and mastering weren't as seamless and as fluid as they should have been. There were places where the sound level wasn't good." Peterson rounded the table.

Secretly, Laurel had thought the same thing. She liked Hall, but the producer and the audio engineer he'd worked with hadn't been as thorough as she'd wished.

"He's given a lot of thought to this. We'd be stupid to turn him down. Your album will automatically get exposure it hasn't gotten in the past. I wouldn't be surprised it if debuted in the top ten on *Billboard,* something that has never happened before."

"I said no, and that's what I meant."

"Alice, please tell your client she doesn't have any choice," Peterson said, his gaze never leaving Laurel's. "It took a lot of rearranging to get the studio and the people he wanted. Not one said no."

They haven't been betrayed and used. Her chin lifted. "All right, but once the album is over, I'm walking. I won't do one thing to promote it."

The man looked pained. "I'm hoping you'll change your mind about staying and about Wilder when you work with him."

"Not likely. Was there anything else?"

Peterson blew out a frustrated breath. "No, I'll see myself out. I'll wait for you in the car, Alice."

A nervous and flustered Alice rushed to her as soon as Peterson left the room. "Laurel, I know you didn't want to work with Wilder, but Peterson is right. This could bring you international fame and put you that much closer to your dream of playing in the Venice opera house."

"The price would be too high. I loathe him," Laurel said and walked to the window. "Start looking for another label."

"Laurel, Arial had been very good to you. Per—"

Laurel swung back around, her gaze narrowed and determined. "Do I need to look for another agent as well?"

Alice gasped, her dark brown eyes widened in alarm. "No. I work very hard for my clients, and you know it."

She did. Alice could be a pit bull on her clients' behalf. "I'm sorry." Shaking her head with regret, she went to the older woman. "Just start looking for another label. Maybe once Peterson finds out, he might relent and I won't have to leave."

The agent perked up immediately. "Great idea. I'll get right on it." Hugging Laurel, Alice hurried from the room.

"Zach, you think you've won, but I'll show you." Her eyes narrowed, she went to phone and dialed.

Eight

Zach knew from the moment Laurel entered the studio Tuesday morning with her two samurai that things were off to a bad start. With her chin high, she looked right through him and warmly greeted the audio engineer, standing a few feet away.

"Good morning, Ms. Raineau," Zach said as if she hadn't ignored him. "I'm aware that you have some reservations about your association with me and my ability to produce an album you'll be proud of. By the time we're finished, I hope to have changed your mind."

"I seriously doubt that."

Silence descended in the studio. People tended to fawn over him. Laurel wasn't the fawning type. At least there were no tears. At least he hoped not. She had on large-rimmed sunglasses.

"Did you have a chance to look over the music I sent over?" he asked.

She placed her violin case on a nearby table. "Since I personally chose the music from my last tour for the CD, I'm very aware of the selections."

Okay, so she deserved to be a diva, but he didn't want Jesse to think she was one. He'd handpicked the crew because they were the best and they knew how to keep their mouths shut once they left the studio.

Only the audio engineer was there today because Zach knew this wouldn't be easy for her. She didn't need a lot of people watching her. Besides, in the pre-recording phase he'd just listen to her rehearse. When he thought she was ready, the actual recording would begin.

"When you want to begin we can run through the first two or three selections so I can get a feel for you."

She stiffened. Her lips pressed together.

Hoping no one had caught her reaction to his bad choice of words, he opened the door to the isolation booth for her, and then went back to sit down at the control panel. "Whenever you're ready."

Opening the case, she removed the violin and went inside the booth. One of the twin samurai closed the door and stared straight at Zach. *Get in line,* Zach thought.

She looked lost. His heart ached for her. He spoke into the mike. "Ready when you are, Ms. Raineau."

For a moment she didn't move. *Come on, honey. You can do this.*

I can't do this.

As long as they were sparring with words she

had been able to push the hurt and, heaven help her, the love away. Now, standing in the booth, aware that he was watching her, she couldn't concentrate.

She'd initially thought to drag out the pre-production sessions until Zachary got the message that under no circumstances would she work with him. Now all she wanted to do was leave quickly so she wouldn't feel the heat, the pull of his eyes.

He'd been polite, formal even, but his eyes—they'd caressed and beckoned. She'd thought nothing he could do would make her forgive him. She'd been wrong—at least partly. It seemed her body could want his even if her mind didn't.

Thankfully, she knew the Tchaikovsky Violin Concerto music by heart. It was her signature piece, and more importantly, she could keep her glasses on to hide her red eyes and puffy lids.

"Take your time, Ms. Raineau. We're here for you."

But I don't want to be here. Positioning the violin beneath her chin, Laurel lifted the bow. The first few notes were fine; then she thought of Zach watching her, the betrayal, and she faltered, stopped. Fought tears.

"Would you like to break and come back after lunch?" he asked.

She thought she heard his voice quiver, much as her body was doing. Foolish of her. He didn't care. He'd used her and now he wanted to make her suffer even more because she had refused him to let him produce her album. But she had freely given him her body.

Hushing the forbidden thoughts away, she shook her head, lifted the violin again, and tried to concentrate. In the past she had always been able to lose herself in her music. It had been her salvation, her solace.

Still her hands trembled. Not this time. She kept seeing Zach, remembering his betrayal.

"Let's take a break."

Laurel lowered the violin, closed her eyes. When she opened them, the other man was gone. Only she, Zach, and the bodyguards she'd asked Rio to send over remained. She'd foolishly thought they would be her shield. She'd been so wrong.

Just being in the same room with him hurt. The pain deepened when she looked at him and recalled how foolish she'd been, how, even now, she couldn't stop loving him.

The door opened and closed. "The sound is off and I told Jesse to give us a few moments. You're just nervous because you're working with a new producer."

"Why are you doing this to me?" she asked, her voice unsteady.

"It was the only way to keep you here. I should have been honest with you, but you have to believe I didn't tell you because I was afraid of losing you. I lo—"

"No. Don't lie anymore."

"Laurel—"

"Please." Her voice trembling, she blinked rapidly to try to keep the tears from falling.

"Do you want to try again in an hour or keep going?"

She lifted the violin. "The quicker this is done, the quicker I'll see the last of you."

"I care about you, Laurel. One day I'll get you to listen."

Laurel began playing before he finished. She didn't want to hear any more lies.

Zach couldn't take watching Laurel struggle for control to play the way she was born and blessed to do. Instead of getting better, she was getting worse. It broke his heart, because he knew he was the cause. He'd taken something beautiful and gifted and ruined it. There were several passages in the Tchaikovsky Concerto where it sounded as if more than one violin were playing. Although it was difficult, Laurel had mastered the piece—until now.

"That's a wrap for today," he said.

Laurel slowly lowered the violin. She opened her mouth, then closed it and started for the door. Her bodyguard opened it and stayed near until she placed the violin carefully inside the case, shut it, and left without a word, the two men following.

"If I hadn't played the CD you sent over, I would think you might be wrong for the first time," Jesse said.

"She's brilliant," Zach said, shutting down the control panel.

"I know, but she's not playing like it." Jesse slapped Zack on the back. "Did you try flowers, jewelry, groveling?"

"We'll start tomorrow at ten." Zach trusted Jesse, but he had no intention of discussing Laurel with him.

"You came through loud and clear. See you tomorrow." Jesse pulled his jean jacket from the back of the chair. "Good luck."

"Bye." Zach would need more than luck. She wouldn't listen, probably hadn't been sleeping or eating. Standing, he toyed with the idea of finding her sister and telling her, then dismissed the idea. Laurel would want to handle this on her own. Suddenly he knew how to get her to eat.

Laurel went straight to her room as soon as the car dropped her off. She started to go to bed, but realized that if she did, she wouldn't get up until the next day. She had to snap out of it, but she had no idea how.

She heard the doorbell ring and hoped it wasn't Sabra. Her mother had a key. Laurel had spoken to both of them last night and reassured them she was all right, that she was going into the studio to start on the new album. Neither asked about the producer, and she didn't tell them. If she had, she was sure both of them would be here.

The phone on her nightstand rang, and she went to pick it up. "Yes."

"Ms. Raineau, there is a messenger here from Mr. Peterson. He says he has to speak to you personally."

"Please show him to the terrace. I'll be right down." Laurel hung up the phone, hurried out of the door and down the stairs. Perhaps he'd heard her agent was looking for another record label and had reconsidered.

She quickly went through the double French doors, her gaze searching for the man. She went down the flagstone steps to the edge of the flower garden with giant flowering hostas beneath the trees. "Hello?"

"Hello, Laurel."

She swung around, knowing she'd see Zachary. Her heart thudded. "Get out."

He held up a wicker picnic basket. "As soon as you eat and promise to take a nap."

"I won't fall for your lies that you want to take care of me again. Get out or I'll call the police."

"And I'll have to call your mother and sister and tell them you're not eating or sleeping."

"You're bluffing. You don't know how to reach them," she told him. She was determined to not involve her family in this.

"Sabra is filming a movie in Vancouver and your mother left for Nashville this morning." Zach removed his BlackBerry from the inside pocket of his lightweight sport jacket. "What will it be?"

"How do you know where they are? Have you been spying on them as well?"

"Both called me the night you left Mexico.

Both made it clear they'd like nothing better than to string me up by my thumbs or worse."

Their calling didn't surprise her. They'd both had strong words for Sean, the singer who had tried to use her. How much worse would it have been if they knew she and Zach had been lovers?

"If I call, my bodyguards will come back and make mincemeat out of you," she threatened, knowing she'd never make the call. She just wanted him to go away so that a small part of her wouldn't desperately want to believe him.

She'd known something was bothering him, but she'd wanted to wait to talk. She shared the blame.

He began to punch numbers.

"Wait!" she said.

He looked up, his thumb poised over another number.

"Hang up," she ordered.

He pressed a button and returned the Black-Berry to his pocket. "Under those trees over there looks like a nice place to eat." He walked to a mosaic table with a padded teak chair shaded by a thirty-foot oak. Opening the basket, he took out a place setting, a glass, and a large plastic container of chicken salad loaded with pecans and cranberries. Finished, he pulled out a chair.

She took the seat and picked up the fork. "You won, now please go."

The corners of his mouth kicked up. "The moment I turned my back you'd go to your room. I'll just wait over there until you finish."

Her fingers tightened on the fork. "What's the matter, Zachary? Afraid word will get out that you've lost your touch, that the album is going to suck?" She'd meant the words to taunt him, but they'd voiced her fear. What if she couldn't pull it together? She desperately wanted to show him his lies hadn't affected her, but each wrong note betrayed her.

The smile left his face. He turned her chair around. He leaned over until his face was inches from hers. "You're the most gifted musician I've ever heard. It was your music that got me through the unexpected death of my father. If you were off today or tomorrow or the day after, it's because I hurt you when I only wanted to love you."

She slapped him. He didn't move, almost as if waiting for her to hit him again. Appalled at what she'd done, she looked away. The lie that he loved her had pushed her over the edge.

He scooted her chair back up to the table and poured her a glass of iced tea. "As soon as you finish, I'll leave."

"I want you gone now," she said, her voice wobbly.

"Then eat," he said from behind her.

Laurel picked up her fork and took a bite of salad. She'd only planned to eat a couple of bites then somehow hide the rest, but she found she was hungry. Small wonder; she hadn't eaten anything solid for the past couple of days.

Finished, she placed the fork aside. "Now you

can leave." When there was no answer, she glanced around and saw the housekeeper coming down the terrace toward her.

Zachary was gone.

In his home office Zachary stared down at Laurel's picture on the cover of her last self-titled CD, *Laurel*. She wore a strapless red ball gown, diamond earrings, and a beautiful, winsome smile. Just by looking at the photo you knew she enjoyed playing and that she wanted to share that gift with you.

He'd ruined that.

Placing the CD aside, Zach went to the window and looked out. He didn't see the riot of flowers and meticulously sculptured lawn and shrubs, he saw the tears in Laurel's eyes.

Tears that he'd caused.

No wonder she had slapped him. She'd opened her heart to him, entrusted him with her body, and he hadn't been honest with her. At the time his reasons sounded good, but looking at it now he realized he had taken the easy way out. He'd been selfish. What he wanted came before what was best for her.

And she had paid the price. Was still paying the price.

His head fell forward. He'd stayed until he was sure she was eating and not faking him out, then he'd left after giving the housekeeper instructions. He deserved the ache in his gut that refused to go away. Laurel didn't.

If she didn't care about him, she wouldn't be struggling to play, and she wouldn't need him to badger her into eating. He knew too many people who gleefully went from bed to bed with irresponsible regularity. Sex was an act, a bargaining chip, a tool.

What he and Laurel had was more than a sharing of their bodies; it was an affirmation of a deeper connection. Passion might have brought them together the first time, but not the other times she'd been with him. She'd cared.

The ringing of his cell phone pulled Zach from his unhappy thoughts. He pulled it from his pocket. "Hello."

"I love you."

He blew out a breath. "Sunshine. You'll never know how sorry I am that I didn't handle this better."

"I think I know," Paige said. "My accusation and tears didn't help."

"I hurt her on so many levels," he said, turning away to sit behind his desk. "I'd give anything to take the pain away, to have the chance to go back and do things differently."

"You love her?"

"Desperately. Hopelessly." He drew in a shuddering breath. "I think she cares as well, but I ruined it."

"Then you'll just have to keep trying to get her to listen, just like Shane did when I refused to listen," she told him.

Zachary sat forward in his seat and recalled

the first time he'd met Shane. Paige was always quiet, somewhat reserved unless it came to the foster children she worked with. He'd expected the same of the man she was madly in love with.

Instead Shane was bold, handsome with a dangerous edge and an unexpected sense of humor. Zach hadn't been sure Shane was the man for his little sister until he saw the way Shane looked at Paige, saw how he understood her better than him or their mother. It was gratifying to know that Paige had finally learned to stand up for herself. He was certain Shane was the reason.

"There isn't anything Shane wouldn't do for you."

"I know," Paige said happily. "I feel the same way about him."

"I'm glad I didn't ruin things for you. The grief I caused Laurel is enough."

"It will help you value what you have even more once you're back together with her."

"I'd give anything for that to happen," he said.

"Then you better get to work and make it happen. Bye."

"Bye, Sunshine, and thanks for the call." Zach hung up and picked up Laurel's CD. "I'm not giving up on us. One day I'm going to tell you I love you and you'll believe me."

"Your guest asked me to clean up when you finished," Judy, the housekeeper, told Laurel. "Your bed has been turned down as he suggested. He thought you'd be tired and want a nap. The

cook is waiting for instructions on what to prepare for dinner.”

“He—” Laurel began, then closed her mouth.
She didn’t know anything about the maid except
she was sweet and cheerful, and came with the
house. The debacle with Zach had taught her
that taking people at face value as she’d always
done could lead to disaster.

She couldn’t let her anger get the best of her
or let any of her staff members know that Zach
wasn’t who he said he was. She had managed to
stay out of the tabloids and gossip TV shows,
and she planned to continue to do so.

She’d take care of Zach tomorrow. If he came
back to her house again, she was calling the police, and he definitely wasn’t ordering her or her
staff around. “I’m going for a walk. You and the
cook can have the rest of the day off.”

“You’re sure you won’t need us?”

“Positive.” He couldn’t tell her what to do!

“Thank you.” The maid moved to clean up the
table. Laurel started to stop her, but decided
against it. Zachary had probably told her where
to send everything. He’d need it for the next
time he tried to soften up a woman. The thought
angered her.

It was anger, not fierce jealousy, she told herself as she started down the flagstone path toward the gardens in the back of the house. She
didn’t want him. Tomorrow she’d show him as
much.

*   *   *

Laurel was positive she was ready for Zach the next day when she arrived at the studio minus her two bodyguards. After a long talk with Sabra the night before while she'd munched on pizza, she had thought of a better way to shield herself from Zach and get a little payback.

He hadn't faked his desire for her, and while men weren't always selective, she couldn't recall a time he had looked at another woman when they were together. He'd had plenty of opportunities with the scantily clad women in swimsuits and sundresses.

She intended to show him what he'd never have again. She wore a floral print mini dress with a tie-detail bateau neckline and three-quarter sleeves. On her feet were red strappy high-vamp sandals with back-zip detail.

If he asked if she'd finished the meal and eaten later—and she was almost certain he would— she'd gladly tell him that she didn't need him pretending to care. She'd gleefully tell him that she'd ordered pizza for dinner, and this morning the cook had prepared her the best omelet she'd ever tasted. He'd remember making her one, and know she'd moved on. She'd sail on by with a smile on her face, leaving behind a subtle yet luscious scent of jasmine and gardenia.

He'd want and know he couldn't have.

She was sure how it would turn out until she opened the door to the area outside the control room. She heard his laughter before she saw him. Her gaze jerked in that direction. Her hands curled into tight fists. A slender young dark-haired woman in a white blouse and black slacks stood close to him. She stared up at him in rapt fascination. They were so caught up with each other that neither appeared to have noticed her arrival.

"R.D., I still can't believe I'm here talking to you," the woman said, her voice a bit breathless with a Boston accent.

"Please call me Zach. I'll be forever grateful for you coming at such short notice," he told her.

Laurel sneered. He'd asked her to call him Zach. She wasn't aware of making any noise, but Zach turned. For once she couldn't read his face. He was as closed to her as Rio.

"Oh, Ms. Raineau. Good morning," the woman said, her hand pressed to her chest. "It's such a pleasure to meet you. R.—Zach said you would be here shortly."

Laurel was thrown off balance by the woman's friendly greeting. Her gaze went from the woman to Zach.

"Ms. Raineau, this is Evelyn Holliday. She's the owner of Holliday Art Gallery and Gift Shop. Ms. Holliday was kind enough to assist me this morning," Zach said.

With the woman still smiling at her, it couldn't have been the way Laurel thought. She extended her hand. "Good morning, Ms. Holliday."

The attractive woman clasped both of her hands around Laurel's, looked at Zach, and then back at her. "I can't believe this. Meeting two of the people on my list in one day." She laughed at Laurel's frown and released her hand. "Ever since I was a little girl, I've always made a list of the people I wanted to meet."

"It must be an unusual list," Laurel said. Then she saw Zach frown and realized she had spoken aloud. She flushed. "I'm sorry. That didn't come out right."

Her face open and friendly, the gallery owner laughed and waved the words aside. "No worry. And you're right. It is an unusual list. Makes life interesting. I have a broad range of interests. Owning a business, you meet lots of unusual and wonderful people. I love your music. I was glad to be able to assist Zach."

Laurel's puzzled gaze went to Zach.

"Thank you again, Ms. Holliday," Zach said, taking the woman's arm. "I appreciate you coming over."

"My pleasure." She laughed. "It helped that you're going to help me scratch several other people off my list. You have absolutely made my day. Heck. My year."

"You helped me as well," Zach said.

"I'll get out of here and let you get to work." She turned to Laurel again. "It was a pleasure. I know the album is going to be a smash hit, and when I listen to it, I'll remember meeting you. Good-bye."

"Good-bye," Laurel said. Still puzzled, she watched Zach walk the woman to the door. They talked a few moments, and then he turned to her.

Silence stretched out as his gaze caressed her. The second her nipples tingled, pushed against the lacy black bra, she realized she had miscalculated. She might be angry with Zach, but her body still wanted him.

She turned away and placed her violin case on the table. "Where is the other technician?"

"Jesse will be here this afternoon. Are you ready?"

"Yes." Picking up her violin, she started for the isolation booth. Out of the corner of her eyes, she saw Zach take a seat in front of the control panel. He hadn't asked one question about her eating. Apparently his mind was occupied with something else.

Opening the door, she walked behind the mike, turned, and went still. She couldn't believe it. On the wall on either side of the glass partition were twelve-foot tapestries of the Metropolitan Opera House. However, instead of the painting showing the stage, it looked from the stage onto the vast audience.

Laurel understood making lists. Carnegie Hall and the Met was on hers, just below the Teatro La Fenice—the opera house in Venice. She'd had one of her best performances at the Met just before she'd left on her European tour.

Her gaze turned to Zach. He watched her.

"Your connection to an audience is fantastic. Look at them. Play for them."

He understood her in so many ways. Perhaps— She left the thought unfinished. She couldn't let down her guard or be swayed by his thoughtfulness. He didn't care about her. He cared about the album. She was just a means to an end. He just wanted to add classical music to his résumé.

She lifted the violin and began to play, then closed her eyes as she missed a note in the Brahms Concerto.

Nine

It hadn't worked.

Zach stayed in the recording studio long after he'd sent Laurel home more than two hours before. He'd called Jesse and told him to be on standby for tomorrow. Zach had wanted to give Laurel the opportunity to lay into him if she wanted for being so overbearing with her, for ordering her staff around. He'd hoped in doing so they'd finally start talking.

Although he'd been ridiculously happy to see her jealous of the gallery owner, it had deepened the wedge between them. She'd looked so fragile. He'd wanted to hold her so badly, he'd trembled. Instead he'd gone to the controls, hoping the mural would do what he hadn't been able to: soothe the ache and steady her.

It hadn't. He hit the PLAY button, looked at the editing screen, and closed his eyes on hearing the screech of the violin, the misery in every note she played. He was making things worse. Opening his eyes, he shut down the control panel and the computer.

He'd see what happened tomorrow. Peterson had texted him fifteen minutes ago, wanting to know how things were going. Zach had no intention of answering the record exec. He was giving Laurel as much time as she needed. He just hoped it was enough.

Hands in his pockets, he left the control room and started outside. Opening the door, he paused on seeing Lee Wilson standing across the street. The anger he'd expected to feel wasn't there. Zach's lies, not Lee, had caused the rift between him and Laurel.

Letting the door close, he started for his Porsche parked at the curb. Lee dodged a couple of cars and crossed in the middle of the street. As he neared, Zach saw that his eyes looked almost wild. He might be egotistical, but Zach had never heard that he used drugs.

"Man, you gotta help me." Wilson clutched Zach's jacket with both hands.

Out of the corner of an eye, Zach saw the security guard for the building straighten. Zach held up his hand. The last thing he wanted was an altercation with Wilson. The media would have a field day. It wouldn't help Laurel think better of him and might make Lee blab about Laurel being with Zach in Mexico. "Take your hands off me."

Lee blinked, almost as if he hadn't known he'd grabbed Zack. He released him immediately and stepped back. "Sure. Sure. I didn't mean anything." He licked his lips. "You gotta tell whoever has everyone spooked that the trip to Mexico never happened. I never saw anyone."

Rio. "I don't know what you're talking about."

"Man, I'm begging. My record company wants to drop me. I can't get into any of the clubs I used to. Even where I bought all of my threads they want cash instead of a credit card. I went to Chauncy's party last night and was asked to leave. My bodyguards left the city." He swallowed. "Tell whoever is doing this that I don't remember anything."

Zach almost felt sorry for the man. Chauncy was a protégé of Lee's. A couple of weeks back they were inseparable. Lee had learned that he wasn't as untouchable or as bad as he'd believed. There was always someone more powerful. "I'll tell them, but it might be better if you made yourself scarce for a month or so."

"I—" Lee swallowed and nodded. "Anything you say. You'll tell them. All right?"

"I'll tell them." Zach got inside his car and watched Lee hurry to his specially built Hummer then climb inside. He was driving himself. The Hummer wasn't filled with men, a woman or two, and blasting loud music. Laurel's reputation was safe, but she was dealing with so much more.

I can't take it another day.

Laurel sat on the bench in the garden of her house and stared at nothing. She'd played worse instead of better today. Her thoughts about Zach were so jumbled and conflicted. She'd been jealous when she saw him with the gallery owner.

But it had been obvious later that they weren't interested in each other. The woman was there to help Laurel. And although at the time she had been sure Zach's reason was self-serving, as the day wore on she saw the strain on his face that deepened with each wrong note she played.

It scared her how much she wanted to believe he really cared. She could feel herself weakening.

He'd looked so tired when he'd told her to call it a day and try tomorrow. She hadn't argued. But she was well aware that she wouldn't play any better tomorrow.

Standing, she went back inside and straight to the phone to call her agent. "Alice, please. Laurel Raineau calling," she said to her agent's assistant.

"Hi, Laurel. How is the recording going?" her agent asked seconds later.

"It's not," Laurel said frankly. "And it isn't going to get any better."

"It's only been a cou—"

"I want you to contact a lawyer to buy back my contract."

"What!" Alice shouted.

Laurel took a deep, steadying breath. "I'll sell everything I own if I have to, but I want out."

"Laurel, you can't. I mean Peterson isn't going to roll over on this," Alice said, a bit frantic. "He's already planning a big announcement about you working with R.D."

"And you didn't tell me?" Laurel asked.

"I knew how you'd react," the agent defended. "Be sensible. This could ruin your career."

Laurel fought the fear trying to consume her. Alice wasn't being overly dramatic. Some of the top music stars had been caught up in legal battles for years over trying to purchase back their music contracts. A legal battle could drain her financially and emotionally. "Do it."

"I certainly hope you know what you're doing," Alice said.

"Good-bye." Laurel hung up the phone. "I hope so, too."

"Laurel Raineau wants to buy back her contract," Peterson said as he entered Zach's home office. There was no effusive smile this time. "I never thought she'd be this stiff-necked."

Zach had pushed and lost, but he'd fight to lessen the fallout for her. "Why don't you give her an extension and, when she's ready, we'll do the album. We both know that album dates are pushed back all the time."

Peterson shook his graying head. "Her lawyer was very specific. She wants completely out. Now."

Zach didn't like the hard look on Peterson's face. "Then let her go. It's obvious that she doesn't want to work with me. You play nice and in a couple of weeks contact her agent. Laurel will remember you didn't hassle her and you can sign her back."

"It's not that easy." He plopped down in a

leather easy chair in front of Zach's desk. "You can't set a precedent in this business and you know it. You try to be nice to one and everyone expects the same treatment. Your ass gets dragged into court for discrimination or vilified in the press."

True. "Then keep it quiet."

Peterson momentarily tucked his head. "Can't. We've already signed two recording artists and promised them you'd produce their albums. Laurel's was the first. If she backs out, news will get around."

"So tell them we had to reschedule because I had a prior obligation," Zach said. "Put the blame on me."

"She's one of our biggest and most prestigious clients. She's one of the few who has played for the president, for sitting kings, queens, and dignitaries all over the world." He massaged his forehead. "There is no way we can keep a lid on this."

The disbelief in Peterson's demeanor was clear. He didn't want to lose Laurel.

"If you fight her, she'll never sign with you again," Zach told him frankly. *And it would shatter her.*

"It's the only way." Peterson's features hardened. "She owes Arial an album and she's going to give it to us or we'll tie her up in court for years."

"What if you had another contract?" Zach asked, not even having to think about what he was about to do.

"What do you mean?"

"An exclusive one with me to produce only Arial artists for two years?"

Peterson's eyes bugged. His mouth gaped as he came to his feet.

"On one condition. That you release Laurel Raineau from her contact at a fair price."

"An exclusive with Arial," Peterson repeated, his expression ecstatic.

"Contingent on you releasing Ms. Raineau and she's happy with the deal," Zachary told him. Laurel's happiness was all that mattered now.

"I'll contact our lawyers right away." Peterson stuck out his hand. "Welcome to Arial."

"Only if Laurel is happy with the conditions for releasing her from her contract. She's not to know about my involvement, either. Otherwise, the deal is off." Laurel wouldn't want him involved, and he couldn't blame her.

"Anything you say," Peterson agreed, his hand still extended.

Zach shook the man's hand. "I think you should deliver the good news personally."

"Certainly. Certainly." Smiling broadly, Peterson practically danced from the room.

Zach watched him go. "Be happy, Laurel. Just be happy."

Taking a deep breath, he went to his desk to call Laurel. There was no sense in her going through the strain of coming to the studio. In a couple of days at the most, he'd be out of her life forever. Just the thought sent a stab of pain through his chest.

Well aware that it would be the last time he'd call her, he slowly dialed her number. And when she answered, it would be the last time he'd talk to her.

"Hello."

His hand flexed on the phone. Yearning mixed with regret swept through at the sound of her voice. Instead of the happiness he'd first heard, there was an unmistakable sadness. His fault.

"Hi, Laurel. It's Zach. Rehearsals have been canceled for the next couple of days. Something has come up."

Silence seemed to go on forever, then, "Good-bye."

His eyes shut. "Good-bye, honey," he said to the droning of the phone, and then dialed Paige. He might as well get all of the bad conversations over with.

"Hello."

"Hello, Sunshine," Zach said, walking to the window to look out. The day was beautiful, the skies blue. He thought of the times he and Laurel had played and made love on the beach.

"Things aren't going well," Paige said.

"No." He blew out a breath.

"I'm sorry. I was hoping you could get her to listen to you."

"I was, too, but that's not going to happen."

"Perhaps she just needs more time," Paige offered.

"Time has run out for us. You can tell Shane and Rio I'll be looking for them. Good-bye." Zach hung up the phone, walked to the stereo system in his office, and turned it on. The pure haunting notes of Laurel playing her violin filled the room.

Head bowed, hands in his pockets, Zachary listened, hoping one day her music would fill the empty place in his heart.

Zach stood on the terrace late the next day with a bourbon and Coke in his hand. He took a sip, remembering Laurel's reaction when he'd called her the day before. He'd thought of little else. Her *Good-bye* meant she had already relegated him to her past.

Peterson's secretary had called that morning to let Zach know that Laurel's attorney was out of town, but planned to return tomorrow. They already had an appointment scheduled. Laurel would have her freedom by tomorrow night. Peterson planned to tell her personally.

His hand clenched around the glass. He wished he could see Laurel one last time, but it would upset her and solve nothing. He'd have to live with the ill-fated decision he'd made, and pray that Laurel could get on with her life. He wasn't sure he could.

Zach heard a sound behind him and looked over his shoulder to see his mother. He wasn't really surprised. From the hesitant expression on her face he reasoned that Paige had called her.

Unlike his father, his mother openly loved her children. Before the debacle he'd created, she would have been across the room with her arms around him by now.

He wanted to hang his head in shame. She'd always been so proud of him. He sat the glass on the table and slowly went to her. "I know you're disappointed in me. I have no excuse."

She cupped his cheek with a hand that trembled. "Zach, I could never be disappointed in you. I love you. Sometimes we make decisions that have far-reaching consequences. I know that better than anyone."

He wanted to feel relief at her words, but there was something in her face, a hesitation that bothered him. "What is it?"

She swallowed. "I have something to tell you. It's something very important. I should have told you long ago."

Fear whipped though him. "You're all right, aren't you? You aren't sick?" he questioned, his entire body shaking with apprehension.

"No, sweetheart." Her hand fell, and she bit her lower lip. "It just that I never could find the right words to explain so you'd understand. With what you're going through, I think you might identify with how things don't always turn out the way we want."

"What is it, Mother?"

"I love you, you know that, don't you?"

He caught her trembling hand. "Mother, you're scaring me."

She glanced behind her. "Trent."

Zach looked up to see a broad-shouldered, brown-skinned handsome man step into the doorway. He was casually dressed in slacks and a long-sleeved white shirt. He didn't speak, just stared at him. Zach's questioning gaze went back to his mother.

"Zach, meet your brother, Trent."

Disbelief, then rage shot through him. "How could Fat—"

She put her fingertips on his lips. He felt her shudder. "Not your father. Trent is my son."

Zach's gaze snapped back up to the silent man who had stepped closer. His eyes were hard until they rested on his mother. "No. That can't be."

"I—" his mother began, then faltered.

"This isn't easy for her. Maybe she should sit down."

Zach wanted to tell the man to get the eff out of his house, but one glance at his mother's pale face and he knew the man was right. "Come on, Mother, sit down. There's water on the serving cart to your left."

Zach helped his mother to a seat on one of the settees on the terrace. By the time she was seated, Trent was there with a glass of water.

"Drink this, Mama," the man said, gently raising the glass to Zach's mother's lips.

Zach wanted to knock the glass away, then plant his fist in the man's face. She was his and Paige's mother. "Paige?"

"She already knows. I told her before she married Shane," his mother answered.

Zach fought a sharp stab of anger. "Why am I the last to know?"

"Don't talk to her that way," Trent snapped, stepping behind the settee to place his big, work-roughened hands on her trembling shoulders.

Zach shot to his feet. "Don't you tell me how to talk to my mother!"

"Somebody has to. She's *my* mother, too," he said, temper flaring in his own dark brown eyes. "You had her all of your life, yet you seem to have forgotten every good thing she ever taught you."

A picture of tears on Laurel's face flashed before Zach. He started for Trent. "You bas—"

His mother's sharp intake of breath stopped him, sliced through him. Trent looked as if he wanted to tear what was left of Zach's heart from his body with his bare hands. Zach knew he deserved it. Trent rounded the chair and sank in front of their mother.

"He's just upset. He's hurt. He didn't mean anything."

Zach felt like slime, lower. His mother hadn't been married when she'd had Trent.

"Mother." He went down on his knees, saw the tears in her eyes, knew his harsh words had caused them. His throat felt tight. No matter what, this woman always loved him, supported him, even when she had to bear the brunt of his father's anger. Nothing would ever change his love for her. He said the only thing he could think of. "I love you. Please forgive me."

She stared down at the glass clenched in her hands.

"Please, Mother, look at me."

He didn't need Trent's sharp elbow in his side to keep talking. "I couldn't be who I am without you. I've made some mistakes, but they were mine. God couldn't have blessed me with a more loving, caring mother."

Her face finally lifted, tears glittering in her eyes, staining her cheeks. He and Trent reached at the same time to brush them away. Each paused, looked at the other, then wiped tears from her cheek on the side where he knelt.

His mother handed Zach the glass, then reached for his hand the moment it was empty. With her other hand, she reached for Trent's. "I dreamed of this moment for so long. I cheated you both out of so much. Trent, you most of all."

"Mama, no. You did what you had to," he said, his voice strained but full of love.

She took a deep breath and stared at Zach. "I just pray you can forgive me when I finish. I was married to your father when Trent was born, but he wasn't your father's child."

Zach's gaze jerked to the man beside him. There was nothing of Zach's father in Trent's dark profile and eyes. Yet he couldn't imagine his mother being unfaithful to his father.

"I met Trent's father a month before the wedding and fell in love." Both of her hands grabbed

Zach's. "It was impossible to call off the wedding. Neither my parents nor your father would have liked the scandal. Trent was born and your father knew he wasn't his and couldn't accept him. I gave him up for adoption and never saw him until he found me." Tears crested in her eyes again. "Trent, I'm sorry I wasn't stronger."

He tenderly kissed her on the cheek. "We've been through this and I hope we don't have to do it again. You had no choice. I have you now." He stared at Zach. A warning. "And I'm not going anyplace."

Silence stretched on and on. Zach tried to process what he'd been told growing up with what he was hearing now. "My older brother died in an accident when her car accidentally ran into the river. Mother was ill for weeks afterward."

"I'm alive. There was no way he would have given her a divorce. Faking the accident was the only solution she could think of," Trent said. "You know how deeply she loves. Neither of us can imagine how difficult it must have been for her to give me up, but it was the only way."

He was right. His mother loved fiercely. His father, on the other hand, had conditions attached to his love. He would have never accepted a child who wasn't his. Zach could only imagine his father's response to Trent's birth. "How did Father react afterward?"

Zach thought he saw her flinch before she said, "We managed."

Zach frowned. His father wasn't the forgiving type, Zach could attest to that.

"If you'd like for us to go, we will," his mother said, her voice shaky.

"He doesn't." Trent stared at him. His eyes promised more than an elbow jab if Zach didn't snap out of it and say something. "He knows how it is when things spiral out of your control through no fault of your own. Loving a person sometimes creates more problems."

He did, but this . . . this was *his mother*. A woman with more honor and unselfishness than anyone he knew. "Trent, help me get Mother some tea." Without waiting for an answer Zach got to his feet and headed for the kitchen. He heard Trent whisper, "Don't worry." Zach gritted his teeth.

In the kitchen Zach prepared the tray for the tea, then turned to Trent, who stood a few feet away from him with his arms folded. Zach didn't want Trent in his house, but tossing him out would only hurt his mother. "You don't look anything like my mother or anyone in her family."

"I take after my father, Wade Taggart. He was a Texas rancher. He met Mother when he went to Atlanta on business."

Zach didn't want to think about his mother with another man. "So you're a rancher."

"I own a trucking company," Trent answered.

If Paige knew about Trent, then Shane knew. He'd certainly have had Trent checked out, but

Shane could have missed something. "Some trucking companies have taken a hit in this economy."

"Not mine," Trent answered, his gaze steady.

Zach pushed away from the counter and walked until he was a foot away from Trent. "Let's cut to the chase. What do you want?"

"What you've had all of your life. My mother. And you and nobody else is going to keep her from me now that I've found her," Trent said, his voice low, each word precise.

Zach could easily recall the warmth and love in his mother's voice and face when she looked at Trent. "Did your adoptive parents help you find her?"

"I grew up in an orphanage."

Zach's stomach twisted. His gaze jerked toward the terrace even though he couldn't see his mother, then to Trent. Learning that must have hurt his mother deeply. "I—I don't know what to say."

Trent shrugged his wide shoulders. "It's over. I have a mother just like I always prayed I would."

"And now that you have a mother?"

"I'm going to do everything in my power to keep her happy," Trent said. "She wants all of her children to know one another. I want what she wants."

Zach picked up the porcelain teapot and turned on the tap of instant hot water. Finished, he placed the teapot on the tray and picked it up. "I'll give you the benefit of the doubt, but if you do one thing to hurt her, I won't rest until I make you pay."

"I'd expect nothing less, but if I wanted to cause problems, I would have done it long ago," Trent said. "But let me warn you, *you* cause Mama any more distress and you'll have to answer to me."

Any more—the words didn't sit well with Zach. He loved his mother. He wasn't about to judge her. He certainly didn't want to hurt her. Nodding abruptly, he returned to the terrace.

His mother stood the instant Zach and Trent returned. She quickly went to them. Her anxious gaze searched their faces. "Is everything all right?"

"Yes," Zach answered. "We were just getting your tea."

"But he forgot the lemons," Trent said.

The fact that he had forgotten his mother liked lemon in her tea, and Trent remembered, irritated the hell out of Zach. He plopped the tea service on top of the glass coffee table. "Perhaps you'd like to go get some."

"Zach, is that any way to talk to your brother."

Zach whirled. A tall, stunning woman with long black hair, in a white pantsuit, stood in the doorway.

"Dominique, you were supposed to wait," Trent said, but there was no heat in his tone. Just the opposite—there was indulgence and love.

"You know how I am about you and your mother." Her eyes locked on Zach, she stopped within a foot of him. "I'm your sister-in-law, Dominique." Her stance combative, she crossed her arms across her chest.

He started to say he didn't have a brother, then clamped his teeth together. He didn't want to upset his mother again, but these other two pushy people were another matter. "It's customary and polite not to intrude on a private conversation."

A perfectly arched eyebrow lifted regally. Her arms slowly dropped to her side. "When it comes to the man I love, the rules don't apply. But after what you did to Laurel, I wouldn't be so quick to point fingers."

Zach's eyes narrowed in anger. Suddenly Trent was in front of him, his dark eyes hard and unforgiving.

"Trent," his mother said, going to him. "Zach might be angry, but he'd never hit a woman. He's not like—"

Zach whirled, rage almost choked him. "Did his father hit you?"

His mother looked startled for a moment, then smiled. "Wade was the gentlest man I've ever known."

Zach saw the love and truth in her face, the wistfulness in her voice. "Where is he?"

She swallowed. Trent and Dominique went to stand by her side, both sliding an arm around her waist. "He died before Trent found me."

Zach's fingers tenderly touched her face with his fingertips. "I'm sorry."

"There's hope for you yet," Dominique said.

Zach's eyes narrowed. "You talk a lot."

She laughed. Amazing as it was, so did her husband, who had been ready to take Zach's head off when he thought Zach might hurt her. "Wait until my cousin arrives."

Zach didn't plan on meeting her cousin or any other relative.

"Don't go stubborn," she said, somehow guessing his thoughts. "Since I stood in your shoes, I'll give you the benefit of the doubt. I know how it is when lies come back to bite you on the backside and make the person you'd give your life for walk away."

"I was a stupid fool," the man said, lifting his hand to lovingly stroke her hair. "If I hadn't been so stubborn, you would have never gotten hurt."

"But it brought us together," she said softly. "Like you, Zach, I had reasons for not telling Trent my real name. My family is wealthy, my brother wealthier. I wanted to make it on my own. When Trent found out my real name was Dominique Falcon, he didn't take it so well."

"Falcon," Zach said. The name rang a bell. "Are you related to Daniel Falcon?"

"My brother. By the way, Trent's cousin, Madelyn, is married to Daniel," Dominique said with meaning. "If that isn't enough, Blade and Daniel, once friendly business rivals, are now close friends. Sierra is the cousin I mentioned. If you weren't Paige and Trent's brother, you'd be over your head in trouble."

Zach was surprised by the connection, but he'd never reacted well to threats. "They know where to find me. They can't do any more to me." His fingers speared through his hair. "Laurel won't talk to me. She won't even look at me. I called the recording off because she looks ready to crash. Nothing they do can make me feel worse. Let them try. I don't care. I already called Paige to tell Shane and Rio to bring it on."

"It twisted my insides when I learned Dominique's true identity and that she hadn't been entirely honest with me, but I was thinking of a past betrayal," Trent told him. "Laurel probably feels the same way. She's hurt."

"No matter what our reasons, we violated Trent's and Laurel's trust," Dominique said. "Love has to build on trust."

Despite everything, they were baring their past to help him. "I know that. Each day we were together in Mexico I tried to tell her, but I was so afraid of losing her. I planned to tell her the last night we were together, but that loud-mouthed Lee Wilson tracked me down and started calling me Rolling Deep. Rio ensured his silence. At least he's not on Laurel's record label, so after I sign the exclusive contract, I won't have to work with him."

"I thought you were a free agent," Trent said.

"He is," his mother said. "He likes the freedom of being able to choose who to work with."

"So what changed?" Dominique asked.

Zach's first thought was to tell them it was none of their business, but it was. With his lies, he had dragged all of them into the situation. It was obvious the family and extended families were close. "The CEO was threatening to sue Laurel if she didn't finish the album. He wouldn't consider letting her buy the contract back. He was going to let it drag on for years."

Zach's lips flattened in a straight line. "She can't stand any more. He wouldn't listen when I asked him to give her more time or release her from her contract, so I used the only bargaining chip I had."

"You."

He looked at his mother. "She's near the breaking point and I put her there. The thought is never far from my mind. I'd do anything for her."

"How do you think Laurel will feel when she learns what you've done?" Dominique asked.

"She'll never find out. It was the only way," he said. "Sometime tomorrow afternoon she'll receive a personal call and then a visit from the CEO. She and the record company will part on amicable terms. She'll be able to return to Nashville and forget."

"I would have never been happy without Dominique," Trent said, and put his arm lightly around Zach's shoulders. "I don't think Laurel will be happy without you. We'll just have to find a way to get her to listen."

Zach didn't even think of throwing the arm off. He wanted Laurel back in his life more than his next breath. "How?"

Trent smiled. "Just leave it up to your big brother."

Ten

A little past seven that night Laurel lay curled in her bed, but at least she wasn't crying. She hadn't known a person had that many tears. Her eyes and head hurt, but still they had come. She cried for Zach's deception, but also because she wanted to believe him. Her arms ached to hold him, her lips to kiss him.

The phone rang on the bedside table. She ignored it. The housekeeper would pick it up.

She didn't want to talk to anyone—unless it was the CEO calling to tell her they'd reconsidered and were letting her out of her contract. Her lawyer said they sounded amicable, but he also said you never knew until you started going over details.

Hope surged through her as the phone rang again. Perhaps it was her lawyer calling again. She rolled and picked up the phone. "Hello."

"Laurel Raineau, please."

"This is she." Her CEO always had his secretary put his calls in.

"Hello, Laurel. This is Paige Elliott, Zach's sister."

Laurel was unprepared for the stab of misery at the mention of his name, the yearning that grew with each breath.

"There's something that I think you should know," Paige continued.

Alarmed, Laurel sat up in bed. "He isn't hurt, is he?"

"Not physically, but he's miserable without you."

Laurel's hand clenched on the phone. "He brought it on himself with his lies."

"He knows that better than anyone, and regrets it more each moment you're apart."

Laurel swallowed the knot in her throat and wondered how long before the aching loneliness dulled.

"He hurt you, and the only way he could think of to set you free is to give up his own freedom," she said.

"I'm not following you," Laurel said instead of hanging up. She shouldn't care what happened to Zach.

"The only way your record company would let you out of your contract without taking you to court was for Zach to sign an exclusive contract with them."

"What!" Laurel came to her feet.

"Zach would have my head if he knew I'd told you, but we decided you should know. No matter what happened, Zach loves you."

Laurel wondered fleetingly who *we* were, then began to tremble when she heard his sister repeat, "Zach loves you."

"He used me so I would let him produce my next album." Laurel paced the length of her room.

"Zach appreciates and loves your music. This might sound pompous, but he doesn't *need* to produce your album. Even without his income from the music industry, he's quite wealthy on his own. Producing your album was personal to him. Your music company's quick capitulation to you shows how well he's thought of in the music industry. He can name his own price."

Laurel didn't have to think long to know Paige was right. Peterson had been salivating over Zach doing the album and getting him to work with other clients on their label.

"If you want to talk to him, we're having dinner at his place tonight. We sort of barged in on him. He needed us, but he needs you more." Paige gave her the address. "I'll leave instructions at the gate for you to get in. Don't let pride and anger stand in the way of the love of a lifetime. Think back to those magical moments when you first met and let your heart guide you."

"He lied to me," Laurel said.

"By omission and because he was afraid of losing you."

"He still lied," Laurel repeated, her voice breaking.

"Not when he said he cared," Paige told her. "Good-bye."

Laurel held the phone in her hand, heard the dial tone, slowly hung it up, and then went back to lie down in bed, drawing her knees up into the fetal position.

He'd lied to her.

You make me want to be better.

I'd rather hold you than sleep.

You're the only woman for me.

The tears started again. She didn't want to be used again. What was she going to do?

Zach couldn't believe he'd let them barge in on him. He loved his mother and sister, but he wanted to be alone. He wasn't fit company.

Even now, he sat at the head of the dining room table slouched in his chair, his chin propped on his open palm, his elbow on the padded arm of the chair. He hadn't even attempted to eat the steak and lobster his chef Kim had prepared. No one seemed to mind. He had to admit he hadn't seen his mother this happy since Paige's marriage to Shane.

There had been a few tense moments when Shane and Paige arrived earlier that afternoon. Paige had shaken her head at him, hugged him, and murmured words of comfort.

Shane had simply said, "You look as bad as Rio said. Good thing, too."

The man was as hard as Zach remembered— unless he was looking at or holding Paige—but as Zach had told Trent, whatever they did to him, he couldn't feel any worse.

Trent. My big brother. Zach might have rejected the arm and the offer of help if he hadn't seen the happy tears in their mother's eyes. He'd simply reached for her. She'd come, clutching both men to her, murmuring over and over, "My sons. My sons."

His mother sat to his immediate right, Paige next to her. Trent sat to his left. When Dominique pulled out a camera, it was all he could do not to ask her to put it away.

"Oh, Dominique, thank you," his mother said, pulling Zach and Trent to either side of her.

"You know I wouldn't forget." Dominique lifted her Nikon. "You can add them to the other pictures. Smile, Zach. This is a momentous occasion."

He'd tried to smile for his mother. He understood how important this was to her. Earlier Dominique had pulled him to one side and explained that his mother didn't want anyone outside the family to know Trent was hers. She didn't want Paige or Zach hurt by cruel gossip.

Zach felt his temper spike again as it did then. She'd sacrificed so much for her family. His father had been a hard, unforgiving man. He wouldn't have let her forget. Yet she'd stayed with him even after her parents died, leaving her a wealthy woman in her own right. She'd stayed for Zach and Paige.

He straightened. "Dominique, if you'll trust the housekeeper with your camera, I'd like one of my whole family. That includes you."

She flashed him a smile and came to her feet. "I have a tripod and timer in my bag."

Trent swallowed, cleared his throat. "Dominique is pretty laid-back unless it comes to her cameras. She doesn't let anyone else handle them."

"She's famous for her photography," his mother said. "Where should we stand?"

"By the open terrace door," Dominique said, setting up the equipment. "Trent, you on one side of your mother. Zach, on the other, with Paige beside you. Shane beside Paige. I'll stand beside Trent. Ready." Dominique hurried to Trent's side. "On the count of three. One. Two. Smile. Three."

The flash went off.

Zach tried to move, and couldn't. Standing in the doorway was Laurel, looking beautiful and weary. He started for her.

Laurel held out her arms to keep Zach from touching her, but he kept walking. He crushed her to him, his body trembling—or was that hers? Her eyes closed as memories and need and, yes, love, washed over her.

"My heart," he murmured, his mouth pressed against her hair.

Tears she'd promised not to shed filled her eyes, then rolled down her cheeks. "You lied to me," she murmured, hearing the anger, the betrayal in her voice.

Lifting his head, he took her face in his hands

and stared down at her. "I'm paying the price. Nothing has been the same for me since the night you walked away from me. But most of all, seeing the tears in your eyes, the disillusionment, is worse than anything I've ever gone through. I'd give anything to go back and make this right. Each tear in your eyes is like a dagger in my heart."

She felt more tears slide down her face. She pressed her lips tighter together. If she tried to speak, she'd start bawling.

"Please don't cry, honey. Please." He kissed her forehead. "Somehow I'll fix this. I promise."

Out of the corner of her eyes she saw two women pass her. Laurel abruptly stepped back. She'd seen them when she came in but, as usual, when Zach touched her, everything else faded. "I didn't mean to interrupt." She turned to leave.

"No!" The cry of distress as much as the hand on her wrist kept her from taking another step. "No," Zach repeated.

Her gaze went to his and stayed.

"If you leave, I'm not sure I can go through another night knowing you're lost to me. I can't."

Indecision held her still. The tortured soul standing before her wasn't the same self-assured, decisive man she'd met in Mexico or dealt with in the studio. He was in pain and openly showing it.

"Hello, Laurel. I'm Joann Albright, Zach's mother. It's a pleasure to meet you."

Laurel jumped and turned to see a striking woman with Zach's eyes. Automatically, she took the hand offered. "Mrs. Albright."

"I'm Paige Elliott, his sister, and this is my husband, Shane," the woman beside her said, extending her hand.

Ingrained politeness made Laurel shake hands with Zach's sister and her husband. She noticed that another couple kept walking.

With one hand still holding hers, Zach caught the arm of the man leaving. "This is—"

"A friend," the man finished. "Trent Masters. This is my wife, Dominique."

More handshakes. Laurel felt a bit disoriented. "I didn't mean to disturb your dinner."

"You didn't," Mrs. Albright said. "Perhaps you can get Zach to eat. I'll ask his chef to bring you both fresh plates when I'm on my way out."

"In the meantime, we have to be going or we'll be late to the theater," Dominique said.

"Good-bye," Mrs. Albright said, briefly hugging Laurel, then smiling at her. "I've waited a long time to meet you. Thank you."

A lump lodged in Laurel's throat.

Paige stepped forward and gently touched her arm. "He was lost without you."

Laurel snuck a peek at Zach. He looked as miserable as she felt. "Served you right," she said, then clamped her hand over her mouth.

Laughter filled the room. She flushed with embarrassment and looked away from Zach, but not before she saw the slight tilt of his mouth upward.

"You'll do," Shane said.

"She certainly will. Let's get out of here," Trent said, reaching for the door and urging everyone from the room.

"Wait," Zach called. "You're all coming back to spend the night, aren't you?" Before tonight his mother, Paige, and then Shane had always stayed with him when they were in town.

His mother blinked rapidly and reached for Trent and Paige's hand. "Yes."

"But not until late," Trent said meaningfully. "We'll call."

Zach understood the subtle message. They'd give him his privacy and time to talk. Somehow Trent had gotten her there. He just might make it as a big brother after all. "Thanks. See you all later," he told them and then turned to Laurel. He wasn't letting go of her until she listened and forgave him.

"Good-bye," Laurel said, still looking a bit weary and dazed. He wasn't sure what she had expected or how Trent had gotten her here; he was just grateful he had.

"Come on, let's go outside." Not waiting for her to answer, Zach walked onto the terrace with Laurel's hand still in his. It felt so good just to hold her, smell her sweet scent. He took the winding brick path leading to the plunge pool. With each step he realized the area with palm tress, dense ferns, and flowering shrubs reminded him of Playa del Carmen. He just hoped Laurel would remember the love and not the deception.

He stopped at the slate edge of the pool. Water gently glided over the curved edge and flowed into the curved receptacle. His hand flexed, felt hers tremble. In Mexico they'd made love in the pool and on the beach.

He lifted her chin with his fingers. His heart clenched painfully in his chest. Her eyes were closed, but tears still seeped from beneath her lids. "Baby, no, please." Gathering her in his arms, he kissed her forehead, her cheek. "I never meant to hurt you."

"You did."

He flinched at the pain in her voice. "I know, and saying I'm sorry isn't enough. But I'd like to explain." When she didn't say anything, he picked her up, felt her tense, and sat with her on one of the lounge chairs facing the wild tangle of trees and bushes that dropped over the side of the steep hill at the back of his house.

He refused to think this would be the last time he'd hold her. "The first time I heard your music was shortly after my father's death. I was still grieving, still dealing with him calling my music useless noise."

She jerked up to stare at him. "He did what?"

"Called it useless noise." Repeating the words didn't hurt as much as it once had because they had gotten her to look at and talk to him. "He favored classical music."

"Is—is that why you wanted to produce my album?"

She deserved honesty. "Partly. But your music touched something in me, helped me deal with my grief at his loss. The night I first heard you, I immediately downloaded every one of your CDs. Unless I working on a project, that's the only music I play."

She stared at him. He couldn't tell if she believed him or not.

"I want to show you something." Setting her on her feet, he took her hand and went back inside to his office, to his home recording studio, and left her standing in the door of his bedroom while he hit the remote control. Her music flowed out from the built-in speakers.

She frowned, shaking her head when he stood before her. "But you're known for hard-hitting rap."

"It doesn't mean I can't enjoy and appreciate other music."

Her chin lowered, then lifted. "I never thought of myself as being a snob or being prejudiced, but it seems I am."

"You love what you love," Zach said gently. "I've always enjoyed music, from the simplistic tinkling of a wind chime to the intricate classics of Chopin or Beethoven to stirring gospel." He leaned over to whisper. "I cried when Mahalia

Jackson sang 'Trouble of the World' in *Imitation of Life.*"

"So did I." A slight smile touched her lips.

"Come on, let's go downstairs to the dining room." Lacing his fingers with hers, he started back down the black spiral staircase. "We can eat and I can try to explain."

"I'm not hungry," she said.

He stopped, studied the dark smudges beneath her eyes, and tugged her down to sit on the stairs. "Remember when I told you that me being in Mexico was a willful, petulant act of self-indulgence?"

She nodded, and he continued. "I was angry that you'd turned me down without even talking with me or my agent. I was even angrier that you believed all those lies about my reputation with women and used that as a reason not to work with me. I followed you to make you change your mind, confident and cocky that I could." His thumb stroked across the top of their clasped hands. "I shaved my beard so if you had seen any recent photos of me, you wouldn't recognize me."

Her hand reached toward his clean-shaven face. "I never paid that much attention to the pictures of you. I'm trying to imagine with you a beard."

He kissed their joined hands. "The beard stays off. This is the face that captured your attention. I'm not taking any chances. In any case, I told myself that it would be to your benefit so I didn't have to worry about not telling you or Paige the entire truth."

He stared at her, let his fingertips graze her cheek. "Then I saw you and knew I was in trouble. Despite what you might have heard, I have never been involved with a recording artist I was producing."

"What about the ones you weren't producing?"

"I really wish you hadn't asked me that," he told her, then continued, "before I met you, I hadn't been with a woman in over a year."

She glanced away and tugged her hand. His hold tightened.

"I have never gone to such lengths to acquire a client, never cooked for any one of them, never had one spend the night in my bed, never watched one sleep for the sheer pleasure it gave me, never been so scared that I might not see her again."

She stopped tugging and stared at him. "You do have a gift for words."

"I don't want to lose you. I know this is my fault." He kissed her hand. "Peterson rightly thinks you're a fabulous recording artist and doesn't want to lose you. The grapevine says you want out of your contract." His hand trembled in hers. "It's a given that he will let you go in the hope that when you're ready to play again— which will be soon—you'll sign with Arial again. You can then go home to Nashville."

"You want me to leave you?"

Never. It will shatter me. "What's best for you is more important than what I want," he told her quietly. "If I'm lucky, one day you'll believe that."

A smile he thought he'd never see again spread across her face. "I already do."

He jerked her to him, his mouth finding hers. His tongue plunged into her mouth, dancing with hers, tasting her sweetness. Her rounded, perfect breasts pushed against his chest, the firm peaks nudging him. He held heaven in his arms. Finally, he had to come up for air.

"You'll never be sorry for trusting me."

"I better not be." Her face grew serious. "I understand about you wanting to make the album for your father. This will be the first one I've done since I lost my own father." She briefly closed her eyes. "I didn't get to spend as much time with him as I should have because of practicing and touring."

"I saw your father in an interview once. He was proud of both of his daughters," Zach said. "I remember him saying that he was blessed to share his talented daughters with the rest of the world."

She smiled slightly. "I remember the interview. He was a great father."

"Remember the good times you had and be thankful," Zach said. "You were one of the lucky ones."

She nodded. "Thanks for the reminder. And now you need to make a phone call."

Lines raced across his brow. "What are you talking about?"

"You are not signing an exclusive contract with my record label so they'll let me out of my contract."

Surprise widened his eyes. "How did you know?"

"Let's say someone who loves you told me." She came to her feet. This time she was tugging his hand. "I'm starving all of a sudden. I can't imagine you not having a fabulous chef. Let's go see what your mother had him prepare."

"Not so fast." He held both of her arms. "You have a phone call to make yourself."

Her eyes hardened. "I'll stop my lawyer from trying to buy out my contract, but this might be my last album for Arial Records in any case. I used to think they cared about me and my music, but all Peterson and the executives care about is money."

"To give Peterson his due, he does appreciate you and your talent, but he was afraid if he let you out of your contract he'd set a precedent that might cause problems with other artists later on," he told her.

"We'll see," she said, her voice noncommittal.

He shook his head. "How could I have forgotten you could be stubborn?" He kissed her on the lips and pulled her into his arms again. "Just as long as you don't forget I care about you. I was afraid I'd never hold you again."

"I was angry."

"And hurt. No more lies." He lifted his head and blew out a breath.

"What is it?" she asked, worry in her eyes.

"I've never been involved with a woman I'm producing," he said slowly. "It's unethical."

She studied him a long time, slid her arms around his neck, and nipped his lower lip. He groaned. "Are you telling me you're putting yourself off limits until the album is done?" she asked.

His hands bracketed her small waist. He could remember all too well what she'd done in Mexico on the ATV jungle tour when he'd tried to resist her. "Laurel, you're going to kill me."

"Not yet." She started down the stairs, her hips gently swinging.

Zach was caught between a grin and another groan, then started down the stairs after her. His teasing Laurel was back.

Eleven

The chef had prepared steak and lobster. Zach and Laurel took their plates out onto the terrace to eat. A full moon shone overhead. "I want to know everything about you."

She forked in a bite of lobster and swallowed before answering. "You probably already know more about me than most people."

His hand briefly touched hers. "You haven't given that many interviews. I read a music teacher visited your kindergarten class and introduced you to the violin and you didn't want to give it up."

Laurel laughed at the memory and sipped her wine. "Mr. Baskin. Ms. Smith, my kindergarten teacher, was noted for her bell choir. Mr. Baskin was the new music teacher and wanted to introduce all the children to other types of music, so he brought the violin to demonstrate. It fascinated me the way the bow created the sounds, the way he seemed to draw music from the strings when all the sounds I managed were horrible.

I was sure there was some trick to it and I was determined to find out."

He shook his head. "Stubborn. I never would have guessed it by looking at you."

"Determined." Laurel cut her rare steak. "On the way home from school, I begged my father to take me by the music store. The moment the man at the store showed me how to hold the instrument, helped me draw a note that didn't screech and hurt my ears, I knew I wanted to play the violin."

"You did, with passion and fire." He stared at her for the pure pleasure it brought him. "You've played all over the world."

"All except the Teatro La Fenice." She sat back in her seat. "Only a few people know it's my Holy Grail."

"Thank you for trusting me."

"One day I'll play there," she told him.

"You said you'd been to Venice," Zach said. "I thought you were already scheduled."

"Not yet," she said, her voice wistful.

He took her hand and stared into her eyes. "You will, and your family and I will be there to cheer you on." He leaned closer. "However, when we take the gondola ride later in the moonlight it will be just the two of us."

"It might not—"

He squeezed her hand. "It will happen."

"After you mastered the guitar, what was next?" she asked, sitting back with her glass of wine. It was good just to sit there and relax with him. He hadn't said he loved her again, but she accepted they were taking things slower this time. She also didn't know if she was ready to say the words or not.

"Any instrument I could get my hands on," he told her. Picking up his glass of wine, he pulled her to her feet and went down the lit path past the rectangular-shaped pool to a sitting area. "My father was gone a great deal working so I got a chance to practice. Paige never minded all the noise I made."

"Your sister and mother adore you," she said, following him down the path, remembering going to the beach with Zach the first night they met.

"I'm glad my bad behavior didn't make them think less of me," he said truthfully. "I was terrified I would never get you to forgive me."

She stopped on the path. "There was a man. I foolishly believed he wanted to be with me and all he wanted was for me to help him get a contract with my record label. I didn't want to be used again."

Zach's face hardened. "I could tear him apart for what he did to you, then I remember what I did."

She placed her hand on his chest. "I have to be honest. If you had told me who you were, I would have walked and not given you a chance to explain. Things happen for a reason. We're past it and it's what happens from now on that's important."

"Laurel," he breathed, curving his hand around her neck, his fingers tightening to bring her mouth closer. Shaking his head, he stepped back. "You push me to my limits, make me forget."

"Does that include the woman you had the serious relationship with?"

He had to touch her, reassure her. His hand palmed her face as he stared into her eyes. "Yes. You're the only woman for me. She hasn't mattered in a long time."

"You said you weren't what she wanted," Laurel continued. "I can't imagine that."

A smile tugged at his lips. Laurel's face was a mixture of pique and disbelief. "Since my father didn't approve of what I wanted to do with my life, he refused to help me financially. I wouldn't receive my trust fund until I was thirty. She knew it, and tossed the ring back in my face when I proposed."

"She did what!" Laurel exclaimed.

Reluctantly he let his hand fall. "The rejection made me work that much harder to succeed. The first year was rough. My lucky break came when the keyboardist at the club where I worked as a bartender was too drunk to play. I took over for him, and when the lead vocalist learned I could play other instruments and could sing a little bit, they hired me. The single we cut a month later debuted in the top ten of *Billboard* and quickly climbed to number one."

"What happened once you made it? Did you call her?"

Zach didn't want to talk about Carmen, but realized Laurel had a right to know. "No. We both had moved on. We talk now and then."

Laurel grunted. Laughing, he hugged her again and urged her into a cushioned seat. "She has no designs on me. She's just going through a tough time and needs someone to talk to. Trust me."

"I trust *you*," she said pointedly and took a sip of wine. "When did you know you wanted to produce music?"

He sat beside her. "Jimi Hendrix again. I saw a video of him playing and was blown away. I listened to other artists who never came close to his magic. Some, like you, don't need anything but an audience. Others need direction. Playing in the band was just a means to an end for me. I like being behind the scenes."

"There's nothing like being in front of an audience whether it's ten or a thousand. The energy is electrifying," she said.

He kissed her ear, sending shivers racing over her body. "There might be one or two things that might compare."

Closing her eyes, she leaned into him. "You might have a point."

He groaned and took a seat on the chaise across from her. "Sorry. I keep forgetting."

"So do I," she mumbled.

He chuckled. "You make life fun again. I missed that. Missed you."

"Then why are you sitting over there?" she questioned, placing her glass on the side table.

"To stay out of trouble. You're too tempting and I'm too weak around you. So please behave," he told her and scooted back farther in the chaise.

She would. For now. "So you think I need direction?"

He placed his glass on the side table and moved forward again, his voice animated. "I've heard you at a live performance and—"

"What! When?" she asked, scooting forward. She hadn't liked that the only time he'd ever heard her play live had been her poor performance in the recording studio.

"At the Metropolitan Opera and in Boston," he told her. "You held the audience in the palm of your hand. You were mesmerizing."

"Thank you," she said, thrilled and excited. "But not on the album?"

He didn't hesitate. "The last album you recorded is good, but if I close my eyes while listening to it, and I have, it doesn't compare to either live performance."

She made a face. "I know. I like Hill, the producer, and although the albums have sold well, I haven't been completely satisfied with the finished products."

"I want to change that." He held out his hands, and she placed hers immediately in his. "There are places the tempo and beat are off, the other instruments competing with you. I have some ideas."

She was suddenly excited. This wasn't just a passing thought, as she'd imagined.

"I had the murals installed because I thought they would help you forget I was there and you could concentrate on the audience," he admitted to her. "It will now."

She didn't need murals. She had something that touched her just as deeply. Him. She looked up at him through a sweep of lashes. "I was jealous of her."

He grinned. "I know, and it gave me hope."

She made a face. "Just like a man."

"That's your man, if you please." Chuckling, he pulled her to her feet. "Let's go inside and make the phone calls to stop all the legal moves."

"Once we do that, we'll be back on track to make the album and it will be official," she said slowly.

He frowned. "It's what you want, isn't it?"

Pulling her hands free, she sat back on the chaise and tucked her head, her hands folded in her lap. As she'd calculated, he sat beside her.

"Laurel, honey, what is it? Whatever it is, I'll make it right. You just have to tell me."

"You promise?"

"I promise."

Her head came up and she reached for the buttons on his shirt. His hands caught hers.

"Laurel, no. I've done enough to you."

"I've cried more tears than I knew were possible when I thought you didn't care, ached for your arms around me, your lips on mine. Do you mean to tell me that you're going to send me home aching and wanting you? That I have to wake up and go to bed the same way for the next four weeks until the album is completed, then another four weeks until it's released?"

He groaned and tucked his head, but his hands stayed wrapped around hers.

"I'll play better."

She heard a strangled sound, felt the shaking of his body. "I'm sorry, Zach, we don't have to. I don't want to upset you."

His head lifted. He was laughing. "Don't ever change."

Nudging his hands away, she began to unbutton his shirt. "No pressure, but since this has to last, you better make it memorable."

"With you, there's no other way." Kissing her briefly, he pulled the dress from her heated body.

His heart stopped on seeing her bathed in moonlight, wearing a lacy pink bra that lovingly displayed her lush breasts, the tiny V of cloth that cupped her woman's softness. He gulped and pulled her back in his arms, his mouth finding hers again, then moving slowly to the curve of her neck, to the slope of her breast. He released the bra.

Bending her over his arm, he pulled her taut nipple into his mouth, ran his tongue over the point, and suckled her. She quivered in his arms. Her fingers gripped his hair. None too steady, he placed her on the chaise and followed her down.

He worshiped her, touching and tasting, until both were quivering with desire.

"I can't wait," she breathed.

He reached into his pocket for the wallet and the condom he'd put there when they were in Mexico. She helped put it on. He gritted his teeth to maintain control. Slipping his hands beneath her hips, he brought them together. She clenched around him. The feel was exquisite.

He began to move, surging into her velvet heat. Her breathing grew more and more ragged with each thrust. She met him stroke for stroke.

She whimpered. Moaned. Enjoyed.

He felt her body tightening beneath his and increased the pace, his powerful body surging into her satin heat, taking them closer and closer to the point of no return. The powerful release hit them at the same time. Their cry of ecstasy echoed through the night air.

Their lovemaking had been memorable. Laurel still felt boneless as Zach opened her front door and they slipped inside. Since she didn't turn on the huge crystal chandelier overhead, the foyer remained in dim shadows with only the light from the two gas lanterns on either side of the twelve-foot glass door.

"I wish you could come in and stay awhile," she said.

His hand tenderly stroked her cheek. "You know what would happen."

"I guess."

He chuckled softly. "I think it's a given. We've called everyone. We're back on schedule. We're in business mode."

She sighed. "I'll see you in the morning."

"Get some sleep. It's going to be a long day at the studio," he told her. Unable to resist, he pulled her into his arms again.

"I don't mind. I'm ready and energized." She ran the tip of her finger over his bottom lip.

He shook his head. "Please behave tomorrow."

She tilted her chin and looked imperious and regal. "I'm Laurel Raineau, the perfect southern lady, in case you've forgotten."

"I could never forget one glorious thing about you." His mouth descended.

Light flooded the room. Zach jerked away, automatically shoving Laurel behind him, thinking that somehow a photographer or an intruder had gotten into the home. His gaze searched the room and he saw a slender woman on the staircase.

It was worse.

He'd know Laurel's mother anywhere. She wasn't smiling as she'd been in the few pictures he'd seen of her. He hoped he wasn't flushing with embarrassment. He certainly couldn't pick Laurel up and rush her back outside to see if all of her clothes were in place. There was only one way to proceed.

"Good evening, Mrs. Raineau. We haven't met. I'm Zachary Wilder."

"Mother!" Laurel came from behind him and ran up the stairs to the woman, who hadn't moved.

"Mother," Laurel repeated. She wrapped her

arms around her mother, seeming to forget that
her hair was mussed. Thank goodness she'd worn
a dress with twists and pleats that didn't look
like it had been tossed atop a bush.

"Laurel," her mother finally said pleasantly
enough, but her narrowed gaze stayed on Zach.

He slipped his hands into his pockets and
tried to appear the innocent instead of the man
who had just made love to her daughter. Twice.
He stared down at his feet.

"When did you get here?" Laurel asked, stepping back to stare up at her mother.

"About an hour ago. You didn't answer your
cell phone and the housekeeper didn't know
where you were." Frowning, she brushed her
hand over Laurel's disheveled hair.

Zach's head came up and saw the motion,
saw Laurel bite her lips. In her happiness to see
her mother, she'd apparently forgotten what
they'd been doing. "The top was down on the
Porsche," he said and wanted to squirm when her
mother's expression didn't change.

"I'm sorry, Mother, that you were worried,"
Laurel said. "I didn't know you were coming."

Mrs. Raineau finally smiled. "Regardless of
what you or Sabra said, you needed me. I stayed
away as long as I could."

"You remind me of my mother," Zach said.
"Her children always come first."

"How does she feel about what you did to my
Laurel?" she challenged.

"Mo—"

"No, Laurel. She has a right to know." He went to the bottom of the stairs. "She said she wasn't disappointed in me, but I know she was. Just as I was in myself. She taught me better. There were reasons for my actions that Laurel knows, and thank goodness, she understands and forgives me. I just hope one day you and Sabra will be able to forgive me as well."

Mrs. Raineau looked at Laurel, then at Zach. "They tell me that you're from the South."

"Yes, ma'am. Atlanta." He didn't know where the conversation was leading, but he planned on remaining respectful. Laurel loved her mother, and that meant it was important that she at least like Zach.

"Then perhaps you're familiar with sitting hens. They might look docile until you try to mess with one of their eggs, and then they'll attack, no matter how large the opponent. They'll protect what's theirs until their last breath."

Zach came up the rest of the stairs until he was a couple of steps below. "I wouldn't expect any less. I messed up once, I won't do so again. She means too much to me."

"Words are easy," Mrs. Raineau said.

"Mama," Laurel said. "He means it."

Zach saw it would take more to convince her mother. He didn't blame her. "Would you like to come to the recording studio tomorrow? I can send a car for both of you."

After a moment's hesitation, she said, "Yes."

"The car will be here at nine thirty. If that's all right?" Zach asked.

"We'll be ready. Good night."

"I'll show you to the door," Laurel said, but her mother caught her hand.

Laurel looked at him with regret and said, "Good night, and thanks for dinner."

"Good night, Laurel, Mrs. Raineau." Zach went down the stairs and out the door. It seemed he wasn't out of the woods yet.

"Mother," Laurel said, looking longingly at the closed front door. "I should have walked him to the door."

Her face lined with worry, Laurel's mother turned her around. "That man made you miserable. Are you sure you should let him back in your life?"

Laurel smiled in reassurance. "Very. He didn't tell me his real name because I was so adamant that I didn't want to work with him. If he had, I wouldn't have listened, and I would have missed getting to know him."

Her mother brushed her hand over Laurel's hair. "But you would have also missed being hurt."

"What I gained is so much more," she said softly, staring again at the closed door. She loved Zach, and when things settled down, she was going to tell him.

Her mother pulled her into her arms. "Oh, my baby. If he hurts you again . . ."

"He won't." Circling her mother's waist, they started up the staircase. "You'll see tomorrow. Zach has my best interests at heart."

"We'll see," her mother said as they continued up the stairs.

"Laurel, I'm at the front door," Zach whispered into his cell phone an hour later. "Can you come down?"

"Let me get dressed. I'll be right there."

Disconnecting the call, Zach waited on the edge of the steps, away from the revealing lights by the double doors. Laurel's gate was coded instead of staffed, so he hadn't had any problems getting back onto the property. He frowned at the thought. If he could get in, so could anyone else.

The door eased open and Laurel, in slacks and a blouse, stepped onto the porch. "Zach?"

"Here." Going up the steps, he took her hand and went back to where he'd been waiting. "Perhaps you should have your gate staffed. Anyone could get back in once they have the code."

She frowned, then curved her arms around his neck. "Sabra is way ahead of you. The code was changed once we were settled and all of the services had come and gone. Rio asked the same thing. Women can think, you know."

He kissed her mouth. "Sorry. I know you're smart. So, how much trouble am I in?"

"A lot, I'm afraid," Laurel said.

"That's what I thought."

"They still see me as the baby of the family. They've always been protective."

His arms tightened around her waist. "My bad behavior didn't help. When I recognized your mother, I didn't know whether to tuck my head or push you back out the door."

"Since things are all right between us, and I was so happy to see her, I forgot." Laurel rested her forehead on his chest.

"The only thing she noticed was the man she thought had hurt her daughter," he told her, hoping he'd been right. He didn't want Laurel embarrassed. "I told you she'd warned me."

She lifted her head and fingered the collar of his shirt. "I think she blames herself a little bit because she went to her class reunion instead of going with me. We've always traveled together."

"I'll just have to show her tomorrow that she can trust me with you," he told her.

Laurel sighed. "She wasn't this upset the last time."

"My guess is that she knows what we feel for each other is deeper. She loves you. My mother . . ." Zach trailed off.

"What is it?" she asked, her voice worried.

"I just thought of a way to help convince your mother I'm not playing a game."

"How?"

"Introduce her to my mother."

"That's a brilliant idea."

"Let's hope so." He kissed her. "Get back inside. I'll see you tomorrow and don't worry."

"I'll try."

"Maybe this will help." He pulled her into his arms, kissing her, hot and possessive.

"You have very persuasive powers."

"Good night, Laurel. Thank you for believing me," he said. "I was lost without you."

"I wasn't much better." She stood there in his arms.

"One of us has to let go of the other."

"I know." She didn't move.

"Laurel."

They both jumped, then laughed. The sound had come from inside the house.

"Mother is looking for me." She went back up the steps. "She probably knows I'm out here."

"It would be my guess. Good night, honey."

" 'Night, Zach." Laurel let herself back inside. Her mother stood at the edge of the entryway.

"Zach?" Mrs. Raineau questioned.

"We hadn't finished talking," Laurel said.

"Hmmm." Her mother started back up the stairs. "Perhaps you should start carrying a comb for these 'talks.' "

Laughing, Laurel ran to catch up with her mother. "I love you. You'll see, Zach is a great guy."

"For you, I want him to be."

Twelve

By the time Zach arrived back home, everyone had gone to bed. They'd told him as much when he left to go see Laurel. All of them, except his mother, had teased and warned him against throwing rocks at the wrong window. He'd held up his BlackBerry, hugged his mother, and left. It had felt good knowing his family was pulling for him, a family that now included a no-nonsense half brother and his outspoken wife.

Since he worked best in the morning, he was up and dressed by seven thirty. He headed to the kitchen for a cup of coffee and a cinnamon raisin bagel to fortify himself until the chef prepared breakfast.

Zach frowned. He had forgotten to tell Kim everyone was spending the night. Hopefully he'd remember his family always stayed, and that by eight thirty all of them were usually down.

He was almost to the kitchen when he heard laughter and voices. Entering, he saw his mother in front of a large griddle, Trent leaning against the counter next to her. Paige was at the stove stirring something in a skillet, and Shane and Dominique were setting the table. The chef was nowhere in sight.

"Good morning. It seems I'm the last to come down."

"Good morning," they greeted him.

"I see you banished Kim from the kitchen again." Zach went to his mother, kissed her on the cheek, and placed a hand on her shoulder.

She smiled up at him, then slid a blueberry pancake off the griddle. "I wanted to cook my children their favorite breakfast."

"What's yours, Trent?" he asked. Quiet descended in the room. Zach knew better than anyone how life took turns you didn't expect. There was no way Trent should ever be considered a mistake or someone to be ashamed of. Somehow they'd find a way for their mother to acknowledge her oldest child. It wasn't fair to either of them.

Trent blinked, swallowed. "Pancakes. Plain."

"Just like me. Paige likes blueberry, as you probably know." Zach went to the cabinet. "I'll get the coffee cups. Anything else I can do?"

"No," Dominique said, brushing beneath both eyes. "You've done enough."

"Glad I wasn't wrong about you," Shane said.

"Really?" Zach said, his voice doubtful as he placed the cups on the table.

Paige laughed and put the scrambled eggs on a platter. "How do you think you got two weeks?"

"What's this about two weeks?" his mother

asked, taking the platter of pancakes to the table.

"Nothing," they all chorused.

His mother, intelligent woman that she was, didn't appear convinced.

"I need your help, Mother," Zach said, well aware that he'd have her undivided attention.

She immediately went to him. "What is it? Is everything all right between you and Laurel?"

"Let's sit down to eat, and I'll tell you."

"Tell me now," she said.

Her stubbornness made him feel buoyant. There wasn't anything his mother couldn't accomplish. "Laurel's mother. She doesn't like me."

His mother's eyes narrowed. Her lips pursed just the tiniest bit. He'd seen that look numerous times in the past—and always when she thought he or Paige wasn't being treated fairly and just before she stepped in to help. "We'll just have to change her mind, won't we?"

Zach smiled and hugged her. He caught Paige's gaze and realized she remembered as well. His gaze unerringly moved to Trent's. Whatever his life had been, it hadn't been with a mother who was always there for him. Zach straightened, his gaze moving around the table. "I might need the entire family on this one."

"That's what families are for," his mother said, taking the seat he pulled out for her.

Zach got out of the Bentley and grinned as he helped his mother and Dominique out of the car, while Toby helped Paige. Trent pulled up behind him in the BMW 750 that was a birthday present from a client. Zach hadn't driven the car more than a couple of times. He'd playfully told Trent there had better not be a scratch on it when he returned. He finally had an entourage, his family.

"I'll go help," Zach said, moving to the open trunk of the BMW where Trent and Shane stood. It had been his mother's idea to have an impromptu brunch when he'd told her that Laurel's mother was coming to the recording session that morning. He wouldn't be surprised if Peterson or Laurel's agent showed up as well.

"People tend to be more social when they're eating or drinking. They feel less awkward," she'd said. The stop at Celebrity Bakery & Café had taken less than fifteen minutes and they were on their way again.

"I'll go with you," Dominique said.

He'd learned that it did no good to try to dissuade Dominique from anything she wanted to do. He was quickly learning Paige had adopted the same self-assured way. She hadn't said anything, just handed their mother her handbag and trailed after him.

"I could help if I wasn't holding handbags," his mother said, shaking her head.

"Gee, thanks." Dominique made a smart turn, draped the strap of her bag over her mother-in-law's shoulder, and went to help.

Mrs. Albright turned to the security guard

staring at Dominique and Paige. "Could you please open the door for them?"

He jumped to open the door. "Yes, ma'am."

With everyone helping, it only took them one trip to take everything inside. It took longer finding a long table to place inside an isolation booth that looked into the control room where Zach would be working. His mother wanted Laurel's mother to be able to watch Zach and see how he and Laurel interacted with each other.

Aware that this was her domain, all of them stood back as she adjusted the ecru tablecloth, then placed matching linen napkins, sterling flatware, flowers, and finally the food. Finished, she stepped back. "On short notice, I think it came out fairly well."

"It's beautiful, Mother," Paige said.

"It certainly is." Dominique shook her dark head. "You always make things appear so effortless."

Mrs. Albright slipped her arms around her daughter's and daughter-in-law's waists. "I've been doing this since I was a little girl. While you were growing up thinking of what you wanted to be, my destiny was already ordained. I was learning the best way to steep tea, how to arrange flowers, and all the other myriad things needed to be the perfect hostess, wife, and mother."

"It's a good thing you did, but we all know that's only a tiny part of who you are." Zach turned toward the sound of the door opening and wanted to groan. "Excuse me."

Crossing the room, he met Mr. Peterson and the other two executives with him. Peterson had a hard frown on his thin face. So did Morris and Keats. Last night he and Laurel hadn't been able to talk directly to her agent or Mr. Peterson.

"Good morning, Mr. Peterson. Mr. Morris. Mr. Keats."

"R.D., what is going on?" Peterson said. "I just spoke with our lawyer this morning, and heard the message you left on my cell phone."

"Laurel and I have worked through our creative differences and decided to do the album as planned," Zach told him.

"What about the exclusive?" he questioned, his gaze sharp.

Zach folded his arms. "The exclusive was on the condition that Laurel be happy once the negotiations were over for her to be let out of her contract. Since she's staying, it negates our talk of an exclusive."

"Are you sure this time?" Peterson asked.

The door opened again. His heart smiled. "Why don't you ask her yourself?"

Zach purposefully hung back as the three men rushed to Laurel and her mother. He wanted to drink in the sight of the woman who moved him. She was breathtaking. This morning she wore an off-the-shoulder turquoise sheath dress. The turquoise jewelry he still planned to give her would look stunning with what she had on or with nothing but bare skin.

Her slow grin made his body tighten. He

mouthed *Behave* just before Peterson blocked
his view. Probably for the best since her mother
wasn't smiling.

Zach joined them and heard Peterson tell Laurel how pleased he was that the album was going
forward. Seeing her eyes narrow, Zach rushed to
say, "I am, too. It's been a dream of mine for a
long time."

Peterson grinned jovially. "I can't wait to
make the announcement. This is going to be big."

"I already have a marketing plan," Morris
put in.

"Give us a couple of weeks first," Zach said.
Once the word was out, Laurel's life would
change. He wanted to give her time to become
adjusted. "Neither one of us wants anything to
distract Laurel. When people learn that we're
working together, she'll have to deal with the craziness of the fans who tend to follow me. She's
not used to that."

Frown lines darted across Peterson's brow.
"Morris has great ideas. I was thinking of making an announcement this afternoon since you
both say you're moving forward."

"We need to move on this," Keats said. "This
is big news."

Clearly they wanted to box them in. "Laurel
and I are committed to the album, but the announcement would have even more buzz appeal
if, at the time, you had the first single from the
album to release. We could have the announcement at my place," Zach said, upping the ante.

"Your place," Peterson repeated, his eyes widening. "I've never heard of you having a party at your home."

Zach wished he could see Laurel's expression. More proof that he wasn't the party animal she thought. "Then the fact that I am doing so will certainly up the expectation and make the guest list that much more exclusive. But I want the two weeks, and once the announcement is made, Laurel is to be provided twenty-four-hour staffed security at the entrance of her home. That's not negotiable."

"Zach, I don't need all that," Laurel protested.

"My fans can get crazy," he told her. "Why don't we put security in place and if you see it isn't warranted, it can be dropped."

"It might be wise," her mother said.

"Peterson?" Zach prompted.

Peterson's gaze flickered from Laurel to Zach and finally to Keats, the CFO, who promptly said. "There's nothing in her contract that—"

"It's the right thing to do," Zach said, cutting him off. "I like working with people who are prudent. So does Laurel. I know you've thought of a follow-up album because you're a man who thinks ahead."

Peterson got the message. Once the album was finished, Laurel was free to go elsewhere. If the album was a hit, and the possibility was very good, record labels would be beating down her door. "A week and I'll see that it's done."

"A week it is." The album was set to be released

in less than two months. There was nothing on the streets about it, no buzz, no anticipation. Zach planned to change that, so they needed to move quickly.

"I'd like to select the security company, if you don't mind," Laurel said, smiling sweetly up at Peterson. "It would make me feel so much better. I'd just like to say that it's wonderful knowing the company you work for cares more about you than the bottom line."

"It certainly is," added her mother.

Zach coughed to keep from laughing. The women were a great team, stroking Peterson and effectively blocking him in.

"Yes. Yes," he said, blinking as if he wasn't sure what had happened. The two men with him looked almost as stunned. "We pride ourselves on caring for our clients."

"Arial has a great reputation," Zach said. "Peterson, if you don't have to rush off, I'd like to introduce all of you and Mrs. Raineau to my family and friends."

"I'd like nothing better," the exec said. The two men with him nodded their agreement.

Laurel's mother said nothing.

Joann Albright watched Zach approach with the three men, Laurel, and her mother, and easily saw that he had been correct. The smile on Carolyn Raineau's face had faded the instant she saw Zach. Joann understood the protective instincts of a mother and applauded them. She had sought to protect Paige from an unscrupulous man, and when she didn't have the power, she had sought help from another mother who did.

Smiling graciously, she listened as Zach introduced everyone, extending her hand to the men. Glad they didn't try to crush her bones, she offered her cheek for air kisses. "It's a pleasure. Please help yourself to the food. Zach said today might be a long one."

"Let me get you a plate," Paige offered, taking Peterson's arm.

"Coffee or orange juice?" Dominique asked the men with him.

"Arial's stock is up this morning on the market," Shane said.

"It will go higher with albums like Laurel and Zach are going to make," Trent said. "Glad to meet the men who are going to make it happen."

Peterson and the men with him smiled as her family led them to another small table once they had their food. They'd keep them busy while Joann talked with Laurel's mother.

"May I get you a cup of coffee?" Joann asked.

"Thank you," Mrs. Raineau said, her voice frosty. She stared at Laurel and Zach, who paid more attention to each other than the food.

Joann picked up a porcelain cup. "Zach, why don't you and Laurel let Mr. Peterson and the men with him hear her magic?"

"Great idea." Zach reached for Laurel's hand, but then he paused and stuck his hand into his pocket.

"Chicken," Laurel whispered and laughed. Opening her case, she removed her violin, then went into the isolation booth and spoke into the mike. "How about Bach?"

Zach nodded, turning on and adjusting the controls. He spoke into the mike so she could hear him. His mother and the others could hear both of them because he'd turned on the speakers in the room they were in. He couldn't hear them. "Just remember you're on stage. Give me more bow. Make me weep."

"I'd like to," Mrs. Raineau whispered loud enough for Joann to hear.

"He did." Joann stared straight at the other woman.

Just then, a crystal pure note had both women turning toward the glass partition. Laurel, eyes closed, her wrist elegantly arched, was playing. She opened her eyes and stared straight at Zach while she played Bach as it was meant to be played, beautifully, passionately, hitting every note just right, pulling, tugging at the heartstrings. Then the last mesmerizing note hung in the air. She and Zach stared across the space at each other.

Even ten feet away in the booth behind them, Joann could feel the intensity. Her eyes teared. She wasn't sure if it was because of the powerful music she'd just heard, or her happiness to see Zach in love with a woman who loved him back. Joann knew too well how emotions could be one-sided.

"Thank you," Zach finally said, his voice rough.

Laurel smiled.

"The album will set sales records for classical music." Morris grinned, standing with the other executives several feet behind Joann and Laurel's mother.

"It might be the best selling yet for the company." Keats nodded his balding head emphatically.

"I've never heard her play so eloquently," Peterson said, his voice hushed.

"Neither have I," Carolyn Raineau whispered, her own voice unsteady. "If he hurts her again—"

"He won't," Joann told her. "He learned from his mistake and regrets more than you or I can imagine. But who has lived and not made a mistake? I know I've done so."

Carolyn brushed a tear from her eye. "Of course you'd take up for him."

"Not if he were wrong. That's not how you raise a child you're proud to call your own."

Mrs. Raineau jerked her head up.

"I prepared his favorite breakfast this morning, set up this impromptu brunch because he knows you don't like him." Joann smiled sadly. "He wanted his mother, his family, to help."

"Why are you telling me this?" Mrs. Raineau asked.

"Because, as a mother, you know what it is to

love a child, to want the best for them, to hurt when they hurt. You'd do anything within your power to take that pain away."

Mrs. Raineau nodded and stared at Laurel. She had come out of the isolation booth to sit beside Zach as he replayed the song and worked on the editing screen. "I stayed away as long as I could. I expected to find her heartbroken; instead she was standing happily in your son's arms."

"Earlier that evening, before she came to see him, he wouldn't eat. Laurel brought the happiness back into his life."

"The cook reported Laurel hadn't been eating. This morning, she gobbled up the breakfast I prepared for her. Her eyes were shining. She couldn't stop smiling. She was so excited, hurrying me to the car he sent," Mrs. Raineau admitted. "She couldn't wait to see him."

"Zach was up early. For the first time since they broke up, it wasn't because he couldn't sleep. He cares about her."

"He lied about his identity."

"But not about his feelings for her." Joann nodded toward the recording booth. "She can't take her eyes off him and he's not much better. It's out of our hands."

Grinning broadly, Peterson entered the recording booth with the two executives on his heels. "The album is going to set classical music sale records!"

"Bank on it," Zach said, turning around on the stool to face the man. "As long as she can focus on her music and not deal with crazy fans or the media," he stressed.

"Anything you want." Peterson patted Zach's shoulder. "I'll let the board know. Laurel, contact my office with the name of the security firm. I'll take care of it or anything else you think she needs."

"Thanks, Peterson."

"Thank you, Mr. Peterson," she said.

Nodding, he and the two men left.

"If you're ready, we can move on to the next selection," Zach instructed.

She leaned to within inches of his face. "Always."

He grinned and watched her take every step back into the isolation booth. Lifting the violin, she began to play.

"Zach is doing everything in his power to ensure she's protected and her music doesn't suffer." Joann nodded toward Zach. "I've visited a couple of times while he was working, and I've never seen him this carefree and happy."

Zach laughed and hooked up two thumbs as Laurel finished another concerto. "The music you selected is fantastic."

"Glad you agree," Laurel said with a regal lift of her brow.

Laughing, Zach stood and gave a regal bow.

"You're as brilliant as you are beautiful, Ms. Raineau. Next number."

"They're having fun," Mrs. Raineau said.

"Yes."

Mrs. Raineau opened the door to the control room. Laurel lowered the instrument. Zach came to his feet. "Mrs. Raineau."

"You make Laurel happy. I expect you to keep her that way," she said.

"Yes, ma'am. I plan to. Thank you."

She smiled and waved to Laurel. "You played beautifully. I love you."

"Thank you, Mother."

Leaving the room, Mrs. Raineau went back outside. "I'll get a cab back to the house."

"And leave me with all of this food? You couldn't be so cruel." Joann went to the table. "At least have a cup of coffee. Perhaps you and Laurel would like to come to dinner tonight?"

Lines raced across Mrs. Raineau's forehead. "I thought Zach would take Laurel out."

"He probably would if he wasn't producing her album. He has a strict policy of not dating women he's working with," Joann explained.

"They're not going to see each other until the album is finished?" she asked, her eyes rounded in disbelief.

"Not romantically. It's one of the reasons he went back to see her last night."

"I guess she won't need the comb I slipped in her purse then," Mrs. Raineau murmured.

"What?"

"Never mind. I've misjudged your son."

"Zach is a good man. I'm proud to call him my son."

"I can see that now." Mrs. Raineau nodded toward the handbag Joann had placed on a chair. "I see you like vintage handbags."

Joann glanced down at the ecru calfskin Birkin. "It belonged to my mother."

Mrs. Raineau laughed for the first time. "My mother carried the same black imitation leather handbag for years. We purchased her several designer handbags, but she never used one of them."

"My mother had a closet just for shoes and bags. My father loved her and never minded when her clothes ended up in his closet."

"My late husband was the same way about my things. He loved us more than anything."

"And you want Laurel to have that same kind of love?"

Mrs. Raineau looked at Zach. "Yes," she answered. She placed her Jimmy Choo snakeskin beside Joann's bag and picked up a glass. "Would you like some juice?"

"Yes, please." Joann picked up a plate. "Danish or croissant. Or both?"

Both women laughed. Chatting, they went to the other card table, sat down, and waved goodbye to Trent, Dominique, Paige, and Shane as they left the studio.

* * *

Laurel couldn't have been happier, and it showed in her music. She didn't mind the long hours of standing or times when she had to go over a particular section. The music and the rapturous expression on Zach's face were enough. It was almost like after they'd had sex. She giggled as they left the studio late that evening. It was almost seven.

Zach frowned. "What?"

"Since you told me to behave, I can't tell you."

He stopped on the sidewalk. "I wish I could kiss you and then take you someplace where we could be alone."

"You'll get part of your wish since you're picking me and Mother up for dinner at your place."

"I'm glad our mothers like each other." Waving Toby away, he opened the back door for her and then slid in after.

Sighing, she leaned against the plush leather. "I should be tired and I guess I am, but I feel so good about today."

He picked up her hand. "You were incredible."

"Why, thank you." She leaned her head on his shoulder. "Before you protest, you held my hand so this can't be off limits."

He leaned his head against hers. "It probably is since it feels so good, but what the hey."

"My thoughts exactly." She snuggled closer. "I'm calling Rio and asking his advice on a firm for the gate."

"I thought you might." He picked up their joined hands. "I have something I want to give you."

She felt something cool close around her wrist and sat up. Her eyes rounded on seeing the turquoise bracelet she'd admired in Mexico. "Zach."

"I'd planned to kiss you and put these on your ears," he told her.

She saw the chandelier earrings in his hand. She loved him so much. She almost said the words. Each time he was with her, he showed how much he cared. "Why don't you wait and plan on putting them on me once we finish the album."

He slipped the earrings back in his pocket. "Deal."

She placed her head back on his shoulder, hoping that when he did he'd finally tell her he loved her.

The next seven days raced by. Zach and Laurel were in the recording studio every day except Sunday. Most of the time, they agreed on the direction of the music, but she wasn't afraid to question him. The difference between Laurel and Lee was that she didn't think she was always right. He learned that the quickest way to solve the problem was to ask her to play the piece both ways, then listen.

"It's annoying when a person is always right," she said on the last day of recording.

"It's wonderful to be able to work with an artist as talented as you are," he'd countered.

She'd rolled her eyes, and they'd gone back to work. He loved to watch her play, loved everything about her. *So why didn't he tell her?* He wondered as he finished dressing for the party to announce their collaboration. He was 99.5 percent sure she loved him, but that 0.5 percent gave him pause.

She lived in Nashville. He was in LA. Long-distance relationships seldom worked for long. Adjusting his bow tie one final time, he left his room. Absence might make the heart grow fonder, but the cravings of the body got people into trouble.

He started down the stairs. He wasn't worried about either of them cheating. He trusted her and, despite the rocky part of their relationship, she trusted him.

So what was his problem? He stepped off the last stair and headed for the kitchen to check on the food preparations. The problem was, his mind was telling him that the next logical step, at least for him, was marriage. Laurel loved touring. She wouldn't want to give that up, and he wouldn't ask her to. So how did they make it work?

He had friends who said they were in love and continued to date. Others just lived together. He'd never ask her to live with him. Now that he'd had time to think it over, he realized that, to Laurel, loving a person meant marriage. Once he said the words aloud, she'd expect the proposal, and when it didn't come, it would hurt her.

Loving a person might be easy, but making a relationship work was another matter altogether.

Entering the kitchen, he saw Kim working with the extra staff his mother had hired. He stopped to taste the smoked salmon and one-bite appetizers. Delicious. Nodding his approval to Kim, Zach left the kitchen.

His mother had come through for him again, Zach thought as he walked through the house and noted the fresh-cut flower arrangements, the wait staff in black tuxedos near the front door with glasses of champagne. In small red gift bags were MP3 players with Laurel's single. Each departing guest would receive one. Morris had given Zach everything he'd asked for.

"Zach, the gate just called," his mother said as she approached. "Laurel and her mother are here."

"Thanks, Mother." He kissed her on the cheek. She looked beautiful, happy, and elegant in a long beaded citron gown. It was her idea to have the event formal in keeping with Laurel's classical music. "Everything looks fantastic. Thanks for helping out."

"I was glad to do it." She straightened his tie. "I would have been upset if you hadn't let me oversee your first party. Especially one that is so important to you and Laurel. Come on. Let's greet your guests." Together they went to the door.

Toby pulled up just as they walked outside. He drove Zach and Laurel to the recording studio every day. It gave them a chance to discuss the tracks—and with Toby in the front seat, it helped them behave. Toby rounded the car and opened the door. Laurel stepped out.

Air stalled in Zach's lungs. Keeping his hands to himself was going to be difficult tonight.

She was stunning in a strapless turquoise straight gown with a bow on the side. On her wrist was the turquoise bracelet he'd given her. She hadn't worn it since the day he'd given it to her. Her slow grin let him know she expected to receive the earrings tonight.

Yesterday she'd finished the last of the ten songs for the album and, despite the fact that Zach and Jesse had to do the mixing and mastering, which could take seven to ten days, she clearly saw that as the end of her obligations. They'd drunk a glass of wine to celebrate, and then he'd taken her home. Last night they'd talked on the phone, but he hadn't seen her again until now.

He quickly went down the steps and took her hand. "You look amazing."

"So do you," she said. "Good evening, Mrs. Albright."

"Good evening, Laurel. You look lovely," Mrs. Albright greeted her.

"Thank you." Laurel leaned closer to Zach. "I hope you have my earrings."

"I do," he said and turned to help her mother. "Good evening, Mrs. Raineau. You look beautiful."

"Good evening, Zach. Thank you." Mrs. Raineau straightened. She wore a long burgundy gown. "Hello, Joann."

"Hello, Carolyn," Mrs. Albright said. "Guests are already at the gate. I'll greet them while you go inside."

"I'll help." Carolyn went to stand by Joann's side.

"Mother, Mrs. Raineau," Zach said, his hand on Laurel's elbow. "You don't have to do that. They'll find their way inside."

"Yes, I do." Mrs. Albright told him. "From the moment they arrive, I want them to know that tonight will be different. Some won't care, but others will."

Laurel hugged Joann. "Thank you."

"The first car is almost here. Go on in. Your mother and I will take care of this."

"Let's go." Frowning, Zach led Laurel up the steps and into the house.

"What's the matter?" Laurel asked when they were inside.

"I invited some of my friends in the music industry who could help get the word out about your album." He looked back over his shoulder. "Our mothers are not going to know how to handle them."

She frowned. "Rap artists?"

"Yes." He wanted her to see and understand his world, the world she was about to be plunged into. If she didn't like his friends or open her mind to different types of music, he didn't see how they were going to make it. "I hope you don't mind?"

"It's your house and your friends. It will give me a chance to broaden my musical scope." She looped her arm through his. "I know some artists in classical music that I'm not too fond of."

He breathed a sigh of relief. "Thanks."

"I expect to be suitably rewarded later on."

He fingered the earrings in his pocket. "Count on it."

As Zach had known, Laurel's single left the guests spellbound. As he'd also known, there were speculative looks from the guests as they moved around the room together. Only one reporter was bold enough to ask if they were romantically involved.

"It's always been my policy to keep the recording sessions strictly business. Thank you for coming." Smiling, he had kept his hand on Laurel's elbow and moved on.

"The nerve of some people," Laurel whispered, her voice tight.

The question was mild, Zach thought, and it was only going to get worse. Laurel had no idea how vicious and mean people could be. If she stayed with him, she'd find out. In so many ways, she was naive. She'd been sheltered.

"R.D., what an awesome party." The willowy redhead threw her arms around Zach's neck. She didn't seem to mind that he still held Laurel's arm.

Releasing Laurel, Zach removed Venus's arms. "Venus, glad you could come. I'm sure you know Laurel Raineau, the guest of honor, and the reason we're here."

Venus, in five-inch heels, placed her hand possessively on Zach's shoulder, playfully flicked his bow tie. "I want you again."

Zach heard Laurel's sharp intake of breath. "I did Venus's last album," he explained.

Venus, always on the lookout for photo ops and publicity, laughed, looked around to see if anyone important or anyone who could help her career might be watching, then pressed her hand to the valley of breasts that spilled out the purple dress she wore. "You were hard, but it was worth it."

Zach felt Laurel tense beside him and figured it was time to move on. "I'm booked up. Enjoy yourself." He moved away, snagging a glass of champagne from a passing waiter and handing it to Laurel. "Nothing happened before or after."

Laurel accepted the glass, but she didn't drink. "Not because she didn't want it to."

"And that's the reason I won't go into the studio with her again," he told her. "*Access Hollywood* is ready for you. I thought you'd do the piece on the terrace." He stared down at her. "You look perfect, but do you want to powder your nose or anything?"

A frown on her face, she glanced up at him. "*People* magazine and now an entertainment news program. Peterson was right about you."

They stepped outside into the cool night air. Guests were on the terrace and standing around the pool. "It's a means to an end. The important thing is that people hear about your single and the coming album."

"But they wouldn't be here if you weren't the producer."

A few steps outside, people converged on them, wanting introductions, wanting to be seen or hopefully to get in some of the footage several TV news programs were filming. Laurel was gracious and smiling. He wished he could tell if she was annoyed. The reporter at the end of the terrace signaled that she was ready. "Good luck."

"Aren't you coming?"

"This is for you."

She took his arm. "We did this." Without giving him a chance to refuse, she continued to the reporter.

The interview went off without a hitch, and so did the next four. Laurel had never had to be "on" for such a long period of time. She didn't like it, and she hoped it didn't show in her face or body language.

Perhaps because she seldom went to parties, she wasn't used to the people who were obviously there with their own agenda or the women like Venus who thought nothing of propositioning a man while he was with another woman. She was definitely ready for the party to be over, but people were crowded into the den watching *Access Hollywood* and waiting for her segment.

Laurel sat on the sofa. Zach and his mother stood behind her, while Laurel's mother and Peterson and the other Arial execs sat with her.

"The music scene has a new sensation, Laurel Raineau. *Access Hollywood* was granted an exclusive with the talented and beautiful classical violinist and Zachary 'Rolling Deep' Wilder, a renowned record producer whose name practically guarantees reaching gold status. Here's our reporter."

"Ms. Raineau, your music is beautiful and timeless. Your last records have gone platinum. How did the collaboration with R.D. come about?"

Laurel blinked, then smiled. "You'll have to forgive me. I think of him as Zachary Wilder, but regardless of the name, he has a heart for music. It speaks to and touches him. He understands the connection between the artist and the audience, and has a wonderful ear for what works." She made a face. "I had to eat crow a couple of times."

There was laughter in the room and on the TV. "R.D., what do you have to say?"

"Producing Laurel's album was a personal dream of mine. Her music touched me while I was dealing with the death of my father. The world deserves to hear it as well."

Sitting there, Laurel was glad Zach had his mother by his side. Even so, she reached over her shoulder and felt his hand touch hers before his fingers slid away.

"Is that the reason for the name of the album, *A Father's Love?*"

Moisture glinted in Laurel's eyes. She blinked a couple of times on the screen and on the sofa. "I lost my father as well. The album is our way of paying tribute to our fathers and fathers all over the world. They helped us become who we are, and we'll never forget them."

"Thank you." The reporter turned to the camera. "I, for one, will be waiting for *A Father's Love* to hit stores. In the meantime, our listeners can go on our Web site and hear Laurel's first single from the album."

The TV screen went blank. There was silence, then applause filled the room. Laurel hugged her mother, who had tears in her eyes, then Peterson was hugging her.

Releasing Laurel, the record executive got to his feet and picked up his glass of champagne. Everyone had been given a flute upon entering the room. He faced the crowd.

"I've never been prouder to be associated with a project." He beckoned for Zach and motioned for Laurel to stand. Once Zach and Laurel stood on either side of him, Peterson lifted his glass.

"To Laurel, Zach, and *A Father's Love.*"

Laurel sipped her wine, wondering why Zach's mother slowly lifted her glass, and looked angry instead of proud.

"Pay up." Her arms folded, her head tilted to one side, Laurel stood on the terrace of Zach's house. The last party straggler had finally gone home. The caterers and extra staff had soon followed. Toby had taken her mother home, and his mother had retired to her upstairs bedroom shortly afterward.

"Technically the album isn't finished until I've done the mixing and mastering and have a master to send to your record label," Zach said, fingering the earrings in his pocket

"After putting up with pushy reporters and women crawling all over you, I think I more than deserve my earrings now."

Catching both arms, he stared down into her upturned face. He'd hoped to see a teasing smile, but he wasn't surprised when he didn't. "There'll always be those who try to use people or be more interested in what sells."

"But it's not the truth," she countered.

"You can't change what people think. If you let it bother you, it will take away your joy in life." His arms slid around her waist, hoping she'd remember that he'd called her his joy. "Surely Sabra has had to deal with the same thing."

She placed her hand on his chest. "She says it doesn't bother her."

"But she's had years to get that way," he said slowly. "Your associating with me thrust you into the limelight. Although I don't like it that you're upset, it brought us together. You're in my arms and forever in my heart."

She sighed and relaxed against him. "You should have been a poet or a songwriter."

"The words only come because of you, because you're in my arms." He set her away. "I better take you home."

"Not without at least one earring."

Removing one of the earrings, he leaned over and brushed his lips across her cheek, slid to her ear, nibbled, and slipped the earring into the small hole. He straightened. "I've missed kissing you."

"Me, too."

"How about we go out to dinner tomorrow night? I can tell you how everything is going."

Her eyes brightened. "I'd like that."

Taking her arm, he started toward the front door. He needed to show Laurel how crazy his life could get—and just hope she cared enough for him to stick it out.

Laurel was more than ready for her date with Zach when he picked her up. The day had been crazy. People were calling to congratulate her, and to ask for interviews. There were flowers from her record label, flowers from Zach, and two arrangements from people she couldn't remember.

Leaving her estate, she saw several people waiting outside. Two men had cameras and snapped as they passed. She was glad they were in the Bentley instead of the Porsche. "I can't believe this."

"I wish I could say it will go away but, because of your association with me and your album set to drop, I don't think so." He caught her hand. "After last night, you made a lot of people's lists."

"I'm not sure I like that." She glanced over her shoulder to look out the back window of the car. No, that wasn't true. She didn't like it at all.

At the restaurant, they were barely out of the car before cameras were flashing and screaming fans were running up to Zachary for autographs. He seemed to take it in stride, even when one female fan pulled down the neck of her T-shirt for him to sign on her skin.

Inside the restaurant, Zach seemed to know everyone, and everyone wanted to chat. He always introduced her. Some knew her and others obviously couldn't have cared less. She couldn't enjoy dinner because people kept coming over. She declined dessert so they could leave early, but forgot about the gauntlet they had to run to reach the car.

In the Bentley, she leaned her head back on the seat. "Is it always like that?" She couldn't imagine living that way, without a moment of peace.

"Sometimes but, like I said, you get used to it."

Laurel didn't say anything else. She didn't think she'd get used to people always in her face. She liked privacy and quiet time. It suddenly occurred to her that this craziness was Zach's life. If she wanted them to be together it would be her life as well.

*   *   *

Zach had been well aware of the reason for Laurel being so quiet on the way to her house. He'd seen her to her door and made a date for the next night. Her brief hesitation had been telling.

Their date the next night and the nights following were a replay. He took her where he knew they would be seen. Her visibility would get her more press, increase name recognition, and hopefully get more airtime for her single. But it also glaringly showed the difference in their lifestyles.

A week later Toby pulled up in front of a nightclub, a hot spot for celebrities. As soon as they were out of the car, the questions started.

"R.D., what's the story on you and Laurel Raineau?"

"Ms. Raineau, how do you feel about R.D.?"

Laurel stopped abruptly. "I want to go home."

Turning smartly, Zach escorted her back to the car. She didn't speak until they were two blocks away. "I don't know if I can go through this again."

Zach's stomach knotted. "After a while you learn to ignore and accept them. They get worse if you try to evade them. Just smile."

"How can you live like that?" she questioned, her voice slightly accusatory.

"The media can be useful. Your album drops in two weeks. Your picture was in *People* last week for the first time. You've been asked to do covers for three top fashion magazines. Orders are up fifty percent and climbing."

"I don't like this."

He gaze was steady. "It's the life I live. The one you'll have to live because of your association with me if you want your music to reach a wider audience."

"I'm just beginning to realize that. I'm not sure I want to pay the high price."

Unable to look at the bleakness of her eyes, he stared straight ahead and fingered the earring in his pocket. He'd hoped against hope that one day he'd be able to give it to her. He knew now it would never happen.

He was losing Laurel all over again, and this time he didn't think he'd be able to get her back.

Thirteen

Zach was miserable. Wednesday evening, hands braced on the balustrade, he stared out at the gardens at the back of his house. He hadn't seen Laurel in six unbelievably long days.

They'd talked briefly on the phone, but the conversations had always been strained. He hadn't asked her to go out, and she hadn't asked him to come over. He got the impression that she was just waiting for the album to drop, and then heading to Nashville.

It would be laughable if it didn't hurt so much that the lifestyle that had initially made her distrustful of him was the very thing that had eventually torn them apart. Blowing out a breath, he shoved his fingers through his hair. Arial Records was having a release party for *A Father's Love* on Saturday night at one of the hottest nightspots in LA.

He hadn't asked Laurel to go with him because he didn't want to put her in a position of turning him down. The least he could do was let her go quietly. He wasn't what she needed, and she was his heart.

Slowly, he went back inside. Hearing the doorbell, his head came up. He quickly crossed to the door. *Please. Please. Please.* His heart beat out a steady staccato as he swung it open.

"Hello, Zachary, can I come in?" Carmen Simpson-Harris bit her lush lower lip, then dabbed her teary eyes with a silk Hermès scarf.

"What are you doing here, Carmen?" he questioned, not moving from the door. He didn't need any more drama in his life.

"I had no place else to go." She bit her lip again, glanced over her shoulder. "He could have had me followed." She lowered the handkerchief, and he saw the bruise on her cheek.

Anger surged through him. Reaching for her, he gently pulled her inside, then picked up the two large pieces of Hermès luggage. "Carmen, what's going on?"

"Please, can I sit down for a moment? Get a drink?"

"Sorry." Taking her arm again, he led her to the living room and helped her to the sofa. Going to the sidebar, he poured her a whiskey. Carmen might look like a lady, but she liked the hard stuff. "Here."

She grabbed for the glass and downed the drink in one practiced toss of her head of tussled auburn curls. Closing her eyes, her hands curled around the glass.

Taking the seat on the coffee table in front of

her, he removed the glass from her hands. "Carmen, tell me what's going on."

Her long eyelashes fluttered, then opened. He vaguely remembered that, at one time, he'd thought her hazel eyes were the most beautiful in the world. Heck, he thought she was the most beautiful woman. He stared at her and felt empathy for whatever she was going through, but nothing else. His heart was firmly in Laurel's hands. "Carmen?"

"I left Peter, my husband." Her eyes closed again. Tears seeped from beneath the lashes. "I couldn't stand it another second."

"Stand what?" Zach asked, although, after seeing the bruise on her cheek, he had a pretty good idea.

"He—" She broke off and looked away. "I-I tried to be a good wife, but nothing I did pleased him and when Peter is unhappy, everyone in the house pays."

Zach felt rage surge through him. He gently placed his hand over hers. "Did he hit you?"

She tensed, then slowly nodded.

Zach pulled out his BlackBerry. "I'm calling the police."

Carmen frantically reached for it. "You can't! Please. I've tried that before. He's an important man in Atlanta. All it does is make things worse."

"Not this time," Zach told her. "Maybe my brother-in-law can help."

"No. Please. He'll find out and I'll pay. You have to promise me that you won't tell anyone

I'm here," she said, tears falling again. "You're my last hope."

"What about your parents, relatives, friends?" he asked.

She lowered her head. "He has more friends than I do. My parents like him. Please, I just need a place to stay for a few days until I can think straight."

No matter what, his mother would never take anyone's side over her children, regardless of who it was. "You're their daughter. Their only child."

"And Peter controls the money. They wouldn't like the scandal. I'm expendable."

Zach sat back. As harsh as it was to accept, he knew that, to some people, money came before anyone. He stood. The threat of a scandal had certainly made his mother reach a decision she'd regret for the rest of her life. "I'll get my keys and take you to a hotel."

She shot to her feet. Fear widening her eyes. "No, he'll find me. I had to use my credit card to buy my flight here, so he'll be looking in LA."

"LA is a big place."

"So is New York, but he tracked me down six months ago." Her hand went to her cheek. "Please, can I stay here?"

"Here?"

"I know it's asking a lot, but it will just be for a few days," she said. "I just want to feel safe and know that he won't walk in on me and—" She looked away but not before Zach saw the tears in her eyes.

"You can stay here," he said. He'd like to have five minutes with Peter.

"Thank you."

He picked up her luggage. "I'll take you up to the guest bedroom. Mother should be arriving in a couple of days."

Carmen stopped. Her hand pressed against her breast. A five-carat diamond glinted on her finger. Several narrow eighteen-karat-gold jeweled bangles jingled on her wrist. "Here?"

He paused at the bottom of the stairs. "Mother would never betray a confidence."

She placed her hand on his forearm, leaned into him, and stared into his eyes. "I didn't mean to infer that she would. You know how much I admire your mother."

He searched his mind, but he couldn't recall Carmen ever talking about his mother, although she had raved about how smart his father was. Her parents were well off, but they weren't anywhere in the same league as his parents or his wealthy grandparents. It wasn't worth thinking about.

"I'll take you up." Turning, he went up the stairs.

Zach asked the chef to prepare dinner for Carmen, then went to his office. He had three back-to-back albums to produce in the coming months. He needed to get busy selecting music, organizing and scheduling the productions, but he couldn't concentrate. He now knew exactly how off center Laurel had felt.

His BlackBerry rang. He grabbed it off his desk and saw his mother's name. He tried not to be disappointed. "Hi, Mother. What time does your plane get in Friday?"

"How are you?"

He blew out a breath and sat back in his chair behind his desk. She'd picked up that something was wrong by the inflection of his voice a couple of days ago. He'd just told her that he and Laurel were going through an adjustment period. "I've been better."

"Is there anything I can do?"

"No—"

"Zachary." A knock sounded on his door.

"Just a moment, Mother." He lowered the BlackBerry. "Come in, Carmen."

The door opened and she stepped in wearing the tiniest black bikini he'd ever seen—and that was saying a lot. She carried a towel over her arm. "Is it all right if I take a swim?"

"Go on."

She started out, giving him an eye-popping view of her backside, then swung back. "When you're free, can you join me? I don't always feel safe."

"Sure." He held up the BlackBerry.

Waving, she closed the door after her.

"Sor—"

"Is Carmen there with you?"

"Yes," he answered. "She's having some problems."

"What kind of problems that she needs to be

at your house instead of home with her husband or her parents?" his mother asked.

"She told me some things in confidence, Mother. She has no place else to go."

"There are hotels."

"Mother, she's going through a difficult time." He blew out a breath. "Life can kick you in the teeth. If I can help her, I will."

There was a brief pause. "I think I'll come to-morrow, if it's all right."

"You know it is. Let me know when your plane is due and I'll pick you up."

"All right. Good night, Zach."

"Good night, Mother." Zach hung up the cell phone and placed it on his desk. Standing, he headed for his recording studio, joining Carmen the farthest thing from his mind.

Zach's mother called Shane and Paige the mo-ment she hung up from speaking with her son. Carmen was up to no good. Joann didn't listen to gossip, but there were increasing rumors of Carmen cheating on her older husband.

Joann had hurt for Zachary when Carmen broke up with him, but Joann had never thought the other woman was right for him. She was too self-indulgent and too conscious of money and social status. She wasn't adjusting well to her husband's financial problems. But if she thought she was going after Zachary now, she'd picked the wrong man!

Hanging up a few minutes later, Joann went

to pack. She quickly climbed the stairs, her anger growing with each step. Carmen would soon find out that no one messed with her children and got away with it.

Wednesday evening Laurel sat cross-legged on the floor in the living room, the recent newspaper and magazine articles scattered around her. She'd won her first competition when she was seven years old, and her mother had kept a scrapbook of everything. Usually, Laurel didn't mind clipping and helping, but each snip made her miss Zach more.

She blinked, hoping to keep the tears at bay. When she opened her eyes again, she saw a white tissue. She lifted her gaze to see her mother's worried face.

"I've tried to keep out of it, but I've grown to like Zach." She came down on the floor in front of Laurel. "Do you want to talk about it?"

Laurel shook her head and took the tissue. "It won't change anything."

"You two were going out every night, and then nothing," her mother persisted. "Something had to have happened."

Laurel balled the tissue in her hands. "His life is just so much different from ours. Everyone seems to know him or want to. We can't move two feet without a camera in our face or a screaming woman wanting him to autograph a part of her body."

Her mother placed her hand on Laurel's knee. "You know what Sabra had to endure, and since she's making movies, the media attention has gotten worse. With her getting an Academy Award nomination for her last movie, it has intensified."

"I can't live like that," Laurel said.

"Are you sure the media attention is the only reason?"

Laurel's head came up sharply. "What are you talking about?"

"Perhaps all the women bother you most of all," her mother said. "I've watched Zach around you. Women might be watching him, but he's watching you."

Laurel opened her mouth to say she wasn't jealous, then snapped it shut and ran her hand through her hair. "Maybe I am a little jealous, but Zach likes going out all the time. I don't mind it occasionally, but not every night."

"Did you tell him?"

"No. I wanted to be with him and he wanted to go out."

"Did you ever think he might think you wanted to go out?" her mother asked. "During the time you worked on the album until it was finished, you didn't go out once. Personally, I admire him for waiting. Especially knowing how impatient you can be when you want something."

Laurel barely kept from blushing. "It's so different here than when we were in Mexico. Except for a couple of times when I think back that he might have been recognized, no one bothered us."

Her mother brushed her hand over Laurel's hair. "And you fell in love there."

Tears cresting in her eyes, Laurel leaned against her mother's shoulder. "So much it aches. He tried to tell me he loved me once, but I was so angry I wouldn't listen. After we made up, I thought he'd wanted to wait until the album was released. But then we started going out, and I don't know what to think anymore."

Her mother handed Laurel another tissue. "I think you and Zach need to talk."

Laurel blew her nose and tucked her head. "What if he's changed his mind and doesn't know how to tell me?"

"Zach doesn't impress me as the kind of man who can't make up his mind. If you love the man, you have to be strong enough to go after him. Make it work," her mother said. "It won't always be roses and moonlight, but it will be the happiest days of your life. Don't waste a moment of life looking back with regrets."

Laurel instinctively knew her mother was thinking of her father. They hadn't always agreed, but not once had Laurel doubted their love for each other. Love might not be easy, but it was worth fighting for. Laurel finally understood that. "Thank you, Mother." Feeling better and more optimistic than she had in days, Laurel went to the phone and dialed Zach's cell phone.

"Hello."

Laurel straightened on hearing a woman's throaty voice. "I must have dialed the—"

"Were you trying to reach Zachary?" the woman asked.

Laurel's grip tightened on the phone. "Yes. May I speak to him please?"

"He's busy. Can I take a message?"

"Please ask him to call Laurel."

"The little violinist?"

"No, the classical violinist. Good-bye." Laurel hung up the phone, her eyes narrowed.

"What's the matter?" her mother asked, coming to stand by her.

"I think one of those women is at Zach's house."

"What are you going to do?"

"I don't know yet, but I'll think of something. She is not getting Zach."

Zach had misplaced his BlackBerry. He was lost without it, but grateful his mother had thought to call him on the house phone when she hadn't been able to reach him on his BlackBerry. By nine the next morning, they were back home. He was barely inside the house when he heard a scream coming from upstairs.

"Carmen!" Dropping the luggage, he hit the stairs running. He burst into her room, expecting to see her husband or some other threat, and saw her thrashing wildly on the bed. The top of the black lacy nightgown had worked its way up over her breasts. There was nothing underneath.

He quickly crossed the room and jerked the sheet up to her neck. Sitting on the side of the bed, he reached for her arms. "Carmen, you're having a nightmare. Wake up." She made incoherent sounds and kept thrashing.

"Carmen!"

"Do you think slapping her would work?"

Carmen jumped, her eyes flying open at the sound of his mother's voice. She screamed again, threw her arms around his neck, and desperately clung to him. "Oh, Zach. I was so scared. It was horrible."

"It's all right, Carmen." He had to exert considerable force to pull her arms from around his neck. She must have been terrified. He quickly stood, pulling up the sheet that had slipped to her waist and handing it to her.

She shuddered delicately, swept her tussled hair back from her face, and grasped the sheet. "Thank you." Her voice trembled.

"You're safe here."

She touched the sheet to each eye, then looked up at him with moisture still shimmering in them. "Because you're here. I feel safe with you."

"I'll just bet you do," his mother said.

Zach frowned. He didn't understand the irritated tone in his mother's voice. She genuinely cared about people, and had known Carmen's parents before she was born. "When you feel up to it, you can come down for breakfast. Just tell Kim, the chef, what you want."

"Where will you be?" Carmen asked, clutching the sheet to her, but one side slipped to reveal her breast.

"In the studio or in my office," he answered slowly, keeping his gaze on her face. He felt sorry for her, but he didn't want her clinging to him or becoming dependent on him. He planned to call Shane later on that day and see what he could find out about her husband. Once they had the evidence against her abusive husband, Carmen could press charges and it would be safe for her to go home.

"Do you mind if I join you? If it's all right?" Twin tears slowly rolled down her cheeks. "I don't want to be a bother."

He could hardly reconcile the self-assured Carmen he once thought he loved with the cowering woman on the bed. "If I'm not in my office, the housekeeper will show you where the studio is. I'll let you get dressed." Catching his mother's arm, he led her out of the room.

"She doesn't wear very much, does she?" his mother said casually once they were in the hallway.

Zach felt the tips of his ears burn. "I'll get your luggage."

Laurel repeatedly called Zach Wednesday night, but the calls always went into voicemail. By the time she woke up the next morning she had decided to go see him. They were going to talk. She loved him. If she had to be the first one to say the words, so be it.

True love meant trusting the other person completely. Zach wouldn't cheat on her, but that didn't mean another woman wouldn't try to tempt him.

She didn't know who the haughty woman was who'd answered the phone the night before, but Laurel wasn't giving her the opportunity to take Zach away from her just because she was having a few doubts at the moment.

Leaving her bedroom, she ran down the stairs wearing the turquoise bracelet, the one earring, and the outfit she'd worn that day in Mexico when they'd seen the jewelry. "I'm coming after you, Zach."

The doorbell rang when she stepped off the stairs. "Mother, the car service is here. Good-bye."

Moments later her mother appeared at the top of the stairs with a hardback novel in her hand. "Good luck."

"Thanks." Grabbing her tote bag with her white bikini inside, and her hat, she put on her sunshades and opened the door, then abruptly stopped upon seeing Paige, Dominique, and another woman she didn't recognize. "Paige. Dominique. What are you doing here?"

"Helping you keep Zach's old girlfriend from sinking her sharp, conniving claws into him," Paige answered.

"That is, if you care," Dominique said.

"If not, we can leave and I can go shopping."

Laurel's gaze swung from Dominique to a striking woman with long black hair who had just spoken. "And you are?"

A smile curved her beautifully shaped lips. "Sierra Navarone."

"You're the one Sabra called, the one who made it possible for me to stay at Navarone Resort and Spa?" Laurel asked.

"Yes."

Laurel put on her hat. "I'll thank you later. Right now I need to get to Zach's house. I think Zach's old girlfriend is already there."

"She is," Paige said. "Mother called us last night when she learned Carmen was staying at Zach's place. She thought Carmen was up to no good and wanted us to come up and make sure whatever Carmen was planning didn't work. This morning Mother called and told us to hurry and take you over there. She's standing guard until then."

"My car service is on the way."

Sierra grinned and started back down the stairs toward the four-door Aston Martin Rapide. "No need to wait."

"I'm sitting in the backseat," Paige said. "That way I won't have to keep my eyes closed."

"Take the front seat, Laurel." Dominique got into the backseat behind Sierra. "We'll fill you in on the way."

Laurel jumped into the front seat and buckled up. "I didn't like it when Zach mentioned they still talked. She was stupid to give him up, but if she thinks she getting him back, I'll snatch a crook in her neck."

"It seems we won't need Mrs. Albright's Plan B," Sierra said as she slowed for the gate to open.

"What's Plan B?" Laurel asked.

"Shane, Trent, and Blade," Paige answered.

"They were backup if Zach wouldn't listen and the woman proved difficult," Dominique explained.

"She's not getting Zach," Laurel said emphatically, then added with a wry twist of her mouth, "But if she proves difficult, I think we should send in Rio."

Shouts of approval filled the car as Sierra drove through the gate. "Thanks for helping us," Laurel said.

"You're family," Dominique said. "We help each other."

Less than a quarter of a mile farther, Sierra took a curve with the barest decrease in speed. The tires gripped the road.

Laurel looked at Sierra who wore a satisfied smile, then Paige in the backseat. "I see what you mean."

"I drive fast, but I never take chances. I have too much to live for. We all do."

Sierra held up her hand, and the women high-fived.

Zach had a headache. The reason was sitting across from him in his office. Although he felt sorry for Carmen, he was tired of the poor-me tune she kept singing. At least she had on clothes that covered her up, although the dress was so tight he didn't see how she was able to sit. It was a wonder the zipper all the way down the front held. He definitely planned to call Shane.

He frowned. When he did, he planned to ask him if there was a way to locate his BlackBerry. He could have sworn he'd left it on his desk last night. He'd seen Carmen come out of his office, but she said she hadn't seen it. He was expecting a call from the director of the Venice opera house. Laurel would have her dream, even if that dream didn't include him.

The doorbell rang, and his mother sprang up. She smiled for the first time since Carmen had joined them thirty minutes ago. "I'll get it."

Zach picked up the phone on his desk to call the director, wishing again that he knew where his BlackBerry was. He was lost without it. He slowly put the phone down. He was lost without Laurel.

"Zachary."

He glanced up, and Carmen stood in front of his desk. Taking her to a hotel today was looking better and better. "Yes?"

She came around the side of the desk. Her perfume was a strong exotic musk. He was sure it was expensive, but he preferred Laurel's softer, sweeter scent.

"I can't hold it back any longer. I wanted to wait, but then your mother came." She put her arms around his neck. "I love you. I'll do anything to prove it."

He was so startled that for a moment he couldn't move. Reality returned when she tried to kiss him, sit on his lap. He grabbed her arms to keep her from leaning closer.

"Anything," she breathed, her red lips slightly parted in an open invitation.

His grip on her arms tightened. "Carmen, what's wrong with you?"

"I realized my mistake. I should have accepted your proposal. We can be together."

He came to his feet and set her away from him in distaste. "I think you should go pack. I'll have Toby take you to a hotel."

Her fingers reached for the front zipper of her dress. "I can make you change your mind?"

"Not in a million years," he said, fed up with her. "Go pack, or I'll pack for you."

"You heard the man."

Zach looked over Carmen's shoulder at the sound of Laurel's voice to see her with Dominique, Paige, and Sierra. Love and happiness swept through him. He rushed across the room to Laurel.

"We'll talk later." She stepped around him to glare at Carmen. "I don't suppose you told Zach your husband tossed you out of the house for cheating?"

"What?" Zach swung back around. "He didn't abuse you?"

"Oh, Zach," Paige said, shaking her head at him.

"She suckered him, just as Joann thought." Dominique folded her arms. "Caught him at a weak moment and moved in."

"I bet she cried all over him," Sierra said with a sneer. "She better be glad she wasn't clinging to Blade that way."

"Trent, either." Dominique held up her hand, and the other woman slapped it.

"Laurel, I—" he tried again.

"We'll talk, but first there's the matter of a little housecleaning." Laurel walked to Carmen, who was seven inches taller in her heels and twenty pounds heavier. "I believe Zach told you to pack."

Carmen took a few steps back. "If you touch me, I'll press charges."

Laurel smiled coldly. "Who do you think they'll believe? Someone whose husband caught her in bed with a business associate and tossed her out, or four respected women?"

"You wouldn't dare."

Laurel got in her face. "You have three minutes to get your things and get out of this house or you'll find out. I *never* shared. Not even in kindergarten."

Carmen stuck her nose in the air and flounced to the door. "I didn't want him anyway. I can do better."

Paige and Laurel started after her. Zach caught both their arms, but the other two women looked at each other and followed her out of the door.

"It doesn't matter what she said or thinks,"

Zach told them and then faced Laurel. "I love you. I love *you*. You're probably the only person who doesn't know it. I believed Carmen and wanted to help her, but she means nothing to me. You. Just you. It had to be you."

Paige cleared her throat. "Mother thought it best if she wasn't in here. I think I'll join her and then see if Sierra and Dominique need any help with Carmen." Paige slipped out the door, but neither noticed.

Laurel slid her arms around his neck. "My family knows I love you. I've loved you from the first."

"*Aaaahhh.*"

Neither bothered to look up at the sound of the high-pitched scream. "I love you, but I didn't like going out every night," she admitted.

"I don't, either." He placed his forehead on hers. "I wanted you to see how crazy it can be, to learn if you could be happy living this kind of life with me."

Her heart thumped, but she said, "You were testing me?"

"I want you to be happy, even if that's not with me."

Her heart melted. Her head lifted. "My mother helped me realize the media frenzy didn't bother me as much as all the women."

He touched the single earring she wore. "I told you that you were the only woman for me."

"I guess I forgot."

"I'll tell you more often so you won't forget."

His arms tightened around her. "I've missed you. I couldn't concentrate on anything."

"Me, too. I don't want us to be at odds again, but Mother said that's part of a relationship. We just have to make sure we talk and tell each other what we're thinking and feeling."

"Sound advice. I was thinking today that there are a lot of great recording studios in Nashville and it's closer to Atlanta."

She had to swallow before she could speak. "You'd move to Nashville?"

His smile was tender and full of love. "Husbands and wives live together. Will you marry me?"

Tears streamed down her cheeks. "Yes, but you're not moving permanently to Nashville. I couldn't be happy unless you're happy. We'll look at our schedules and work something out."

"You love touring," he said.

"I despise touring. I love playing before a live audience." She kissed his lips. "But it doesn't compare to being with you and in your arms. That's a happiness I refuse to give up or go one day without."

"What about the media? The women?"

"The media is a small price to pay to be with you. As for the women, I'll keep you so happy and satisfied, you'll be too worn out to even look at one," she said, leaning more fully into him.

He moaned slightly. "Works for me."

"In fact, I think we should go out tonight to

remind people about the release party Saturday night. And if everyone can stay, we'll have a get-together just for the family at my house Friday night. My mother and yours would love to plan a dinner party for us," she told him.

"You're incredible and I'm one blessed man." He kissed her, his mouth grazing her ear just before he put the other earring on. "Beautiful. It's finally where it belongs."

"Just like I am."

He kissed the woman who would hold his heart forever.

Cameras flashed, women screamed as Zach stepped out of the Bentley, then reached back inside. Smiling, Laurel emerged, grinning and waving. She leaned over and whispered to Zach. "I've always wanted to do the royal hand-wave thingy."

"It's R.D. and Laurel Raineau!"

"Oh, my goodness, there's Sabra Raineau! She's up for an Academy Award!"

"Is that Blade Navarone? He never goes out!"

"There's Dominique Falcon-Masters! This is huge. Her collection of Native American black-and-white photographs are in the Smithsonian."

Sierra leaned over to Paige. "I guess you, Shane, Trent, Pierce, and I are nonentities."

Blade's arm tightened around her waist. "No, you're my world."

"Same goes." Dominique leaned against Trent.

Pierce kissed Sabra on the cheek as the five couples posed for pictures. "Ditto."

Paige laughed and said, "Ditto for me and Shane."

Shane laughed with her, then looked over his shoulder at the silent and watchful Rio. "Smile."

Rio's expression remained stoic.

Laurel laughed and turned to go inside the restaurant. "Let's go eat."

"Ms. Raineau, what's going on between you and Rolling Deep?"

Laurel glanced over her shoulder at the man who'd asked the question and winked. "Be at the release party Saturday night for *A Father's Love* and find out. But I will say, R.D. is a man of many talents."

Questions were fired at them, but the group swept inside, laughing and talking. All except the silent Rio who followed.

Epilogue

Monday morning Laurel woke up blissfully happy. Wearing only the turquoise bracelet and earrings, she snuggled closer to Zach in his bed.

"How does it feel to have your album debut at number one?" he asked, his hand stroking up and down her bare back. "To be scheduled to play at the Venice opera house?"

"Exciting, unbelievable. I still can't believe either of them. You made all my dreams come true." The album release party had been wildly successful. There had been major print, radio, and TV coverage.

She knew a large part of the buzz was due to their outing Thursday night. She had to admit she'd had fun. It was the people you were with and not the people surrounding you that mattered. Sitting up, she kissed Zach on the cheek. Zach had made the announcement of her scheduled performance at the Teatro La Fenice at the release party. Peterson was ecstatic, and her agent had rubbed her hands in glee.

"But it doesn't compare to this," Laurel finally answered.

"Nothing ever will." His fingers curved around her neck to bring her lips closer. The kiss was long and hot.

The BlackBerry on the nightstand rang. His arm wrapped around Laurel, Zach checked the caller ID, saw that it was Peterson, and shut it off. Paige, Dominique, and Sierra had found his phone in the guest bedroom when they were "helping" Carmen pack.

Laurel sighed with contentment. "Do you think it was a coincidence that your mother invited mine to spend a few days with her and they took off with everyone last night?"

"Do you?"

"No. They knew we wanted some time to be alone." The tip of her finger ran over his lower lip. "I still can't believe we're engaged."

"Maybe this will help." Sitting up, he reached under the pillow and pulled out a black box. Opening it, he removed a square-cut five-carat blue diamond encircled with white diamonds. "I wanted to give you a ring that is as stunning and as beautiful as you are."

"Zach." Her voice trembled as he slid the ring on her finger. "It fits."

"Just like we do, for a lifetime," he said. "When you love and are loved in return, nothing else compares to it. It had to be you."

"We're going to spend the rest of our lives

showing each other. I agree, no one else would do. It had to be you," she said just before he pulled her into his arms and down into the bed.

William H. Ray

FRANCIS RAY (1944–2013) is the *New York Times* bestselling author of the Grayson novels, the Falcon books, the Taggart Brothers, and *Twice the Temptation,* among many other books. Her novel *Incognito* was made into a movie that aired on BET. A native Texan, she was a graduate of Texas Woman's University and had a degree in nursing. Besides being a writer, she was a school nurse practitioner with the Dallas Independent School District. She lived in Dallas.

"Francis Ray is, without a doubt, one of the Queens of Romance."

—*A Romance Review*

DON'T MISS THESE OTHER NOVELS
BY BESTSELLING AUTHOR

FRANCIS RAY

THE GRAYSONS OF
NEW MEXICO SERIES

Only You

Irresistible You

Dreaming of You

You and No Other

Until There Was You

THE GRAYSON FRIENDS SERIES

All of My Love (e-original)

All That I Desire

All That I Need

All I Ever Wanted

A Dangerous Kiss

With Just One Kiss

A Seductive Kiss

It Had to Be You

One Night With You

Nobody But You

The Way You Love Me

AGAINST THE ODDS SERIES

Trouble Don't Last Always

Somebody's Knocking at My Door

THE FALCON SERIES

Break Every Rule

Heart of the Falcon

A FAMILY AFFAIR SERIES

After the Dawn

When Morning Comes

I Know Who Holds Tomorrow

THE TAGGART BROTHERS SERIES

Only Hers

Forever Yours

INVINCIBLE WOMEN SERIES

If You Were My Man

And Mistress Makes Three

Not Even If You Begged

In Another Man's Bed

Any Rich Man Will Do

Like the First Time

STANDALONES

Someone to Love Me

The Turning Point

ANTHOLOGIES

Twice the Temptation

Let's Get It On

Going to the Chapel

Welcome to Leo's

Della's House of Style

AVAILABLE WHEREVER BOOKS ARE SOLD

 ST. MARTIN'S GRIFFIN